With This Ring

After her small son, Kevin, asked both God and Santa for a new daddy for Christmas, and then didn't find him under the tree, schoolteacher Jessica Price is starting the new year out with a very unhappy six-year-old little boy on her hands. He can't understand that she's only been a widow for two years and she can't imagine marrying again. But, unknown to her, Kevin has a plan and has decided that if God and Santa won't give him what he wants, then maybe the police can!

When the very handsome chief of police, Levi Sinclair, shows up as Kevin's show-and-tell, he believes—as does she—that Kevin has asked him there to show him off as the police chief—*it's a little awkward when her son introduces him as his next daddy!*

Things are getting a bit complicated on the shores of Windswept Bay! Come join the fun in With This Ring, book 6 of this captivating series. You've watched the four Sinclair sisters fall in love; now it's time to watch the five Sinclair brothers find the women of their dreams.

WITH THIS RING

Windswept Bay, Book Six

DEBRA CLOPTON

CHAPTER ONE

"Hurry, Momma. Drive faster."

Jessica Price shot a glance in the rearview at her six-year-old son. He was tiny for his age and looked so very small in the back seat. "I'm going the speed limit, young man. What's your hurry, anyway?" She knew what it was, but asked him anyway, glad to see his beaming smile again.

"It's show-and-tell and I have the best one of anybody," he exclaimed, bouncing in his seat belt.

Kevin had been excited ever since the day before when Deputy Ryan Locke, and his wife Jillian, had picked Kevin up and given him a ride in a Windswept Bay police SUV decked out with lights and siren. Kevin had been in heaven.

Ryan had promised him the ride before Christmas. But then Ryan and Jillian got married, and then Kevin had gotten ill. And then the holidays had taken precedence and there just hadn't been time for Ryan to fulfill his promise until yesterday. She'd been thrilled watching Kevin's joy as the man he'd connected with at Thanksgiving had strapped him into the backseat of his cop car and taken him for a ride. She didn't want Kevin to grow up and be thrilled to ride back there but for a little boy, it was one of the most exciting days of his life. It showed in his eyes as he'd looked at Ryan. It had been one more reminder to her that her son had no man, alive, to call Daddy and he so desperately wanted one.

He'd made that clear at Christmas.

But that was a hard thing, because she wasn't ready to think about marrying again. So for Ryan to come through on his promise after the Christmas they'd just had was a huge thing for her as well as for

Kevin.

Ryan and Jillian had given Kevin a ride to the police station for a tour. And it had been there that he'd met Jillian's brother, Chief of Police Levi Sinclair. Kevin had talked nonstop about him.

It was obvious that he, too, had been kind to Kevin because, to her son's delight, the chief of police had agreed to come to the school today to be Kevin's show-and-tell in class.

It was the perfect distraction for him from what had happened over the holidays and seeing Kevin his happy self again made her happy. She would have to thank the chief because it was a welcomed difference from the quieter child Kevin had been since being so disappointed about not getting his Christmas wish. *Her poor son.*

They'd driven from Windswept Bay back home during the two-week holiday to spend Christmas with their family. With a six-year-old and Roscoe, their huge dog, it had been a long drive from Florida to Kansas. The drive must have given Kevin time to come up with his heart-wrenching plan of asking Santa and

God for a new daddy for Christmas!

He'd been one highly disappointed child when a new daddy had not been waiting for him underneath the Christmas tree on Christmas morning.

She sighed even now, thinking about it. She hadn't known how to help him. She wasn't ready to find a husband. Adam had only been dead two years. She needed time…though she certainly didn't want her little boy growing up without a daddy and nor would Adam want that. Her sweet husband had grown up without a dad and knew what it felt like. He would want her to remarry, for both Kevin and herself. But her heart…her heart was not ready.

And so this morning, as she drove to school with Kevin bouncing with excitement, she was happy. Maybe this was the start of a good new year after all.

They'd made it through one more Christmas without Adam, and as hard as it was, she knew they would make it…he would want it that way and he would want her to be strong. And she had been. Taking this job in Florida, so far away from her family, had been part of her determination to move forward. To stand on her own two feet.

She pulled into the parking lot of the school and smiled over the seat at Kevin. "We're here. Are you happy now?"

He grinned as he unbuckled his seat belt. "Oh yeah, this is going to be the greatest day of my life! All my friends are going to be so jealous." He grabbed the door handle.

"Hey, hold on there. You know not to open that door before I get out of the car." Her warning had him stopping before he jumped out of the backseat.

"Yes, ma'am. But could you please hurry?"

She laughed, grabbed her purse and got out of the car. The kid was going to run her ragged before her time.

Levi Sinclair stood outside the elementary school building. His phone rang and he pulled it from its clip on his belt. The ID showed that it was Jillian. He was in this fix because of her. She and Ryan had brought Kevin to tour the office and the cute little guy had been curious and excited and had asked Levi all kinds of questions. Levi had answered every one of them as Jillian and Ryan had stood in the doorway of his office and grinned while they watched. And then Kevin had asked him to come to his class today for show-and-tell. Levi hadn't been able to say no.

"Hey," he said, after accepting the call. His sister's soft chuckle greeted him.

"I called to remind you about Kevin's class this morning, but I can hear the angst in your voice so I'm assuming you're on your way."

He scowled. "I'm standing outside the school now. And stop laughing. You got me into this. You and my new deputy. I think you knew Kevin was going to ask me to do this. As a matter of fact, I bet you and your husband might have set me up."

Jillian chuckled again. "He did ask Ryan to do it when we were riding around in the SUV. But, Ryan just told him that the police chief would really be impressive to show off for his class. And he was right, this is a good thing."

"I'm glad you think so."

"Don't be nervous—you'll do fine."

"I'm not nervous," he denied, but in truth, he was a little. He'd never been comfortable when talking to kids and usually sent one of his deputies for things like this.

Levi liked kids; he just wasn't good with them. Which was why he'd been surprised when Kevin had taken his hand and had him come on the station tour with them. The freckled faced kid looked younger than a first grader and had chattered excitedly the whole time asking all kinds of questions. He had a great sense of humor and had Levi and Ryan laughing several times. There had been no way Levi could say no to helping him out.

"You were great with Kevin yesterday and he really enjoyed the time you spent with him. I just want to say good luck. Kevin needs this attention. And his mother, Jessica, is a sweetheart. You'll meet her. She's one of Kevin's teachers."

"Okay, well, I better get in there."

"Go and have a good time." She laughed and ended the call and he entered the school building.

Immediately Levi was transported back to his childhood, when he had been a student here at Windswept Bay Elementary. He'd been a rebel back then at the ripe old age of six. He and Ryan had, together, given the teachers the dickens. No one would have believed that he—or Ryan, for that matter—had grown up or would grow up to become police officers. Ryan's dad had been the police chief back then, and Mr. Locke and Levi's dad, Sam, had made many trips to the school's principal office to discuss their young reprobates.

Maybe that was the reason Levi had a little trouble coming back here for things like this. What if he saw a kid acting up? What was he supposed to say—*watch out, if you keep acting like that you could grow up to become a police officer*?

He laughed silently to himself as he reached room three. The door was open and he could see colorful tables with children looking toward the front of the room where a little girl was showing the class her turtle. A turtle might be far more interesting to a room of first graders than a police officer. *Poor Kevin; this might be a no-win situation for the kid.* And that suddenly bothered Levi.

Where was the teacher? Levi saw kids starting to notice him in the doorway and decided he needed to lean forward and look past the doorframe in order to see the rest of the room and find the teacher. Instead he waited until the little girl finished showing off her turtle—she reminded him of his sister Shar, who was a one-woman wonder when it came to rescuing endangered sea turtles. Heck, Shar would have been a huge hit for show-and-tell. Levi should have suggested her to Kevin instead of coming himself. The little girl set her turtle back in its box sitting at her feet. And then he started to lean forward, just as a pretty strawberry-blonde woman moved into view. Her blue eyes crinkled at the edges as she smiled at him.

"Hello, Chief Sinclair, it's so good of you to come. Just one moment please."

As she spoke, Levi wondered whether this was Kevin's mother. Jillian had said that she had been at the Thanksgiving Day Celebration that the Windswept Bay Resort his family owned put on each

Thanksgiving. That was where Jillian and Ryan had first met Kevin and his mother. Then later they had rescued Roscoe, Kevin's dog, and returned it to the boy. That was when Ryan had promised to give Kevin a ride in the police vehicle, which had also turned into a tour of the station.

Studying the teacher, Levi realized he had seen her that day at the meal. She had been at the buffet line and he'd noticed then, like he was noticing now, that she had a soft beauty about her. He looked away, irritated with himself. He wasn't here to notice the teacher's beauty; he was here for Kevin. But when she glanced back to him briefly, her expression warm with welcome, he had a hard time focusing on anything but her.

"Class, we've been highly entertained by Clara and her turtle, Jeremiah. Thank you, Clara. You may sit down now."

Levi heard the smile in her voice and saw the twinkle in her eyes. An avalanche of attraction rumbled through him as she turned back to him and held out her hand.

"I am Jessica, Kevin's teacher and his very grateful mother." She leaned close so only he could hear her words. "Thank you so much for coming. It means the world to him. He's been so excited since yesterday when you agreed to show up."

He took her hand and yes, that attraction went up his arm like a forest fire eating up ground before he released her hand. "I'm glad to be here. Your son is quite a salesman."

"Yes, he is. Please, come in."

Levi stepped into the classroom and all the kids could see him now. He spotted Kevin at one of the tables with a look of complete exhilaration on his little face. The boy jumped to his feet and waved.

"Hi Levi-I mean Chief," he called.

Immediately Levi was glad he'd come. Ryan had told him that the boy had lost his father and Levi felt bad for him. "Hi Kevin."

Jessica chuckled. "Okay, Kevin, calm down. It's your turn for your show-and-tell time. I'll let you introduce your guest." And then smiling, she moved to the back of the room as Kevin raced full throttle to the front of the room and looked up at Levi with a gigantic grin from ear to ear.

"I knew you'd come," he gushed.

"Of course I came. You asked me, didn't you?"

Kevin nodded. "I did." He leaned forward and whispered, "I just had to see it to believe it." And then he stared at Levi for a long quiet moment.

"Kevin, introduce him," Jessica urged.

"Oh, yeah," he laughed and took Levi's hand and turned toward the class of about thirty-five.

Levi surveyed the room then. There was another woman at the back of the room who smiled as Jessica joined her. The kids were staring at him with varying degrees of interest and Levi suddenly felt very much like Jeramiah the turtle.

"Today, for my show-and-tell," Kevin said in a very serious tone, "I have brought Police Chief Sinclair. But I call him Levi, because he told me to the other day when he showed me the police station. It was really, really cool. But that's not why I brought him to be my show-and-tell." He grinned and looked up at Levi for a moment before dramatically looking back at the class. "I brought him to show you all that he is going to be my new daddy."

What? Levi nearly broke his neck as he looked from the class of suddenly alert, wide-eyed kids down to the boy grinning proudly at his classroom of peers; then the boy turned his face up and grinned at Levi with an expression of pure delight.

The boy had just told his classroom and his mother that Levi was going to be his new daddy…and he did not look like he was joking. *Where had that come from?*

Levi's gaze met Jessica's. Her mouth was open and she looked as if she'd just been hit with a bucket of ice water—then she turned red and hurried up the row of tables.

But Kevin was talking again, "When he's my daddy, we can all go to the station and he can take us on a tour then lock us all in jail cells and—"

Jessica interrupted him, "Kevin, um, that was interesting," she said in measured tones. "But you may sit down now."

"But, I'm not finished—" Kevin started.

Jessica held up a finger to stop him. "No sir," she said, firm but gentle. "You've had your time."

To his credit, the boy shot one last wistful look up at Levi and then headed back to his seat.

Levi, though stunned, noticed that the kid looked taller as he walked away.

Jessica turned toward him and a pale pink tint stained her cheeks. Her blue eyes seemed to ask for understanding. "I'm sorry," she said softly. "He's going through a tough time right now. I had no idea he planned to do that."

Levi had been trained for all types of trouble. Nothing had prepared him for this…it was awkward to say the least. And sadly a little heartbreaking. He felt for her and he felt for Kevin.

"It's okay," he assured her. "Since I'm here, can I say something to the kids?"

Relief flashed in her expression. "Yes, please, whatever you would like. The floor is yours. The children would be thrilled to hear something from you. And maybe it would distract from what just happened," she said, continuing in the soft tones that they had been speaking in.

"That's exactly what I was thinking."

She turned back to the children who were now talking excitedly. "Calm down, everyone. Chief Sinclair wants to say a few words to all of you. Now please quiet down and give him the respect that he as our police chief and one of the men who protects us and our community deserves."

Levi watched her as she moved aside. She chose not to go to the back of the room this time but instead stood near the doorway.

"I think Kevin may have made a great suggestion for a field trip. I think I'll coordinate with Ms. Price for a tour of the police station for the classes and all of you kids can meet my deputies. That way when you see them on the streets, you will know them and know that they are your friends. And that if you ever need help, you can feel comfortable asking them." He was amazed at how the children stared at him with complete attention.

One of the boys in the front row raised his hand and Levi decided that questions from the kids might be a good option.

"You have a question?" He pointed at the kid; immediately, other hands went up around the room.

The little boy grinned. "When are you getting married?"

And then the questions started.

"When are you marrying Ms. Price?"

"My mom is not going to be happy," a little girl huffed. "She said she was going to marry you, Chief Sinclair. My mom said you were a hot hunk."

"My mama said she bet you kissed good," a little boy said and made a face. "That's gross."

"Class," Jessica gasped.

"Hold on, kids." Levi held up his hand, deciding maybe he should have left when he had the chance. *How many of these kids' moms had talked about him?* He glanced over at Jessica who looked as troubled as he felt.

"Class," she said, her voice tight. "Police Chief Sinclair and I are not getting married. And I would thank you for not spreading this around."

"But Kevin said so," someone declared.

"Yes, he did, but no. We are not getting married."

"I believe it's time for me to go." He told her.

The little girl whose mother had called him a hunk and wanted to kiss him jumped from her chair. "My mom is not going to be happy."

Levi did not even answer; he just got out of there as fast as his shoes would carry him. Show-and-tell had not been a good idea.

Not a good idea at all.

CHAPTER TWO

Mortified, Jessica watched Levi Sinclair stride out of her class without a backward glance. Her spirits plunged a little further down than they'd already plummeted when her son had ambushed the poor man.

"Quiet down, class," she urged.

Lana Presley, her co-teacher in the classroom, had come forward to help regain control of the class. "Okay that's enough kids. It's time to get out your paper and draw a picture of your favorite show-and-tell of the week. I think we've had enough fun for the morning."

When the kids started to talk she backed them down firmly and to Jessica's relief despite a few grumbles they did as they were told.

"Thank you," Jessica said as Lana turned to her and gave her a teasing grin.

"Kids will be kids. So, how does it feel to be marrying the hunky chief of police?" she drawled in her deep Texas accent.

Lana was from a big family and had five brothers back on the ranch in Texas. Like Jessica, Lana had had her own reasons for moving to Windswept Bay—like finding a life that wasn't overrun by all the men in her family. With their similar longing for independence, she and Jessica were becoming really good friends. But she did love to tease, and now was a prime opportunity, it seemed.

"Your humor is not appreciated," Jessica said in a soft hiss.

Lana chuckled and leaned close. "Especially now that you know, according to the kids, that all the single moms in your class have the hunky police chief on their radars?"

Jessica didn't laugh. "This is bad, Lana. What am I going to do? When all these kids go home and start talking, you and I both know rumors are going to be rampant."

"It'll be fine. Stop worrying. I was just teasing and hey, he is handsome. And obviously Kevin likes him."

Jessica gasped. "I'm so embarrassed. Poor guy got ambushed. I've barely settled into life at Windswept Bay and now I'm going to be the talk of the town. But the worst of it is, I don't know what's going on with Kevin."

Lana knew what Kevin had done over the holidays and gave her a sympathetic, "Yeah, that's bad."

"I thought he was doing better since the Christmas disaster but obviously he hadn't forgotten at all. He chose his gift when he met Levi yesterday. That's what he's been so excited about for the last twenty-four hours." She rubbed her temple and the ache that was throbbing there. It was going to be a long day and probably a long week.

Lana patted her arm. "I was just teasing you. As

my daddy loves to say, 'This too shall pass.' Really, Jessica, you're tough and you can endure some gossip until it dies away. And it always does. Of course, the smaller the town, the longer it hangs on…I can tell you from personal experience about that one."

"I believe you. But that still leaves me with, what *was or is* my child thinking?"

"He's a boy who naturally wants a daddy. He'd just got his hopes up. And well, maybe it's a sign that you should start dating. You know, at least try."

Jessica sighed. "I'll do that when I'm ready." She just wasn't sure when that would be.

"What is up with you?" Ryan asked the minute Levi stormed into the police station. Ryan had been Levi's best friend growing up and now was one of his deputies and also his brother-in-law. If anyone knew Levi, it was Ryan.

Levi narrowed his gaze at his friend, the friend who he really thought had set him up on this little ambush. "Do you really want to know what happened?

Because when you brought Kevin in here yesterday and started telling the kid that I was the one he should be asking to do the show-and-tell, I should have known something was up. Did you know something I didn't know?"

Ryan leaned back in the desk chair and grinned. "What is wrong with you? Kevin needed someone for show-and-tell and I just thought the chief of police would be a better choice."

Levi paced the office, looked toward the dispatch office and then he hissed so that only Ryan could hear. "The kid set me up."

"So you think Jillian and I set you up?"

Levi did not hold anything back. "That's exactly what I'm thinking. I think you knew that that little boy wants a daddy really badly. Poor kid."

Ryan's expression turned serious. "Yeah, I kind of knew that. So maybe I did set you up a little. Jessica is a great gal. And I just thought I'd set you up to at least meet her. That's all I was thinking, though. You're both adults. Once you meet, it's between the two of you."

"Well you did a great job," he muttered, the scene

in that classroom replaying in his mind.

Ryan frowned. "Levi, what happened? Why are you acting like this?"

"Because, I was not there to be Kevin's show-and-tell as the police chief. I was there for Kevin to introduce me to his class as his new *daddy*."

Ryan busted into laughter. "He introduced you as his daddy?"

"No, sorry—I'm a little out of it at the moment. He told the kids that I was *going* to be his new daddy. And then all the little kids started telling me that their single mothers were going to be upset because they wanted to kiss me and thought I was a hunk. A *hot* hunk."

Ryan's expression drooped into disbelief. "I had no idea that was going to happen. This is bad."

Levi scowled. "Tell me about it."

Betty Lou, the dispatcher, stuck her head out the door of the dispatch room. "Hey, boss, this could be real fun. Heaven knows you need a wife. You should take the kid up on his offer and marry his mama."

"Betty Lou, don't you have a switchboard or

something to operate?"

The older woman just laughed. "I'll get to that. This was too good to ignore. I'm already surprised you don't get pancakes and love letters dropped off here on a regular basis. You being a hunky dude and all."

"Hey, cut it out."

"You did say all those children's moms said you were hot and hunky. I'm just wondering why none of them brought you baked goods. You know the way to a man's heart is through his stomach. Even one as flat as yours."

Ryan's shoulders shook, he was laughing so hard.

"You two are a barrel of laughs. I think I'll go make some rounds…and get some fresh air."

He was being ridiculous, he knew, but this was not in his job description. And then there was the fact that Jessica had been very attractive. And something about the way he felt when her eyes met his spoke to him— really made him realize that it had been awhile since he had been out on a date. Despite the fact that he had plenty of opportunities he'd been focused on his career.

After this fiasco, it might be a lifetime before he

went out on another date. If there was one thing he did not like, it was the spotlight. He tried to keep his town out of the spotlight and his personal life too.

His gut told him things were going to change…at least for a little while. Maybe there wouldn't be any fallout from this but his instincts were good and they told him this was not over by a longshot.

Jessica asked Lana to watch both classes as she took Kevin out into the hallway. After Adam had passed away, she'd gotten him counseling for a few months but he seemed to be handling things well and they'd stopped. This new obsession with a new daddy had just started within the last couple of months. Until he had asked Santa for a daddy, she hadn't realized that he had become fixated on this new topic. And she had thought that they had handled it until now. In the hallway, she bent down so that she could look him in the eye. He looked at her with expectation in his bright eyes.

"You don't look happy, Momma." His eyes searched hers. "Don't you like Chief Levi?"

There were so many things she could say to him. But what was the right thing to say? Parenting was not easy. Parenting under hard circumstances was even harder and more complex. *What did one say to a six-year-old longing so hard for a daddy that he would do this?* "Kevin, honey, I love you. You know that, right?"

He nodded. "I know you do, Momma."

"Can you tell me why you suddenly want a daddy so bad? You know that when the time is right, I'll find you a new daddy."

That serious expression that made him look so much like Adam came across his little face. "Levi is him. Don't you like him?"

Her patience strained. "Kevin, I don't know him. I just met him today when he came here for you. You can't just tell someone they're going to be your daddy. I know you want a daddy but it's not that easy. So please don't do that again, okay?"

"But—"

Tears of frustration, uncertainty, and anguish welled in her eyes. "No buts. This is a decision you can't make, honey." She pulled him into her arms and hugged him tightly. He squirmed almost immediately and she let him go. "Let's go back in the classroom and finish out this day. Also, remember that tomorrow we are going to go help with the puppy adoption at the park. That will be fun."

"Okay," he said, not sounding convinced.

And she wasn't either. This was too complicated. The only thing she knew at this moment was that she owed Levi Sinclair a huge apology for what had happened and probably for what was about to happen. Thank goodness it was Friday. Hopefully by Monday morning the kids would have forgotten all about show-and-tell and things would move forward.

Did she really believe that? Not for one second, but a girl could dream.

CHAPTER THREE

On Saturday morning, Levi went for his jog along the beach, really glad that today was his day off. It had been a long night. He had dealt with a lot of problems over the years but a little kid doing what Kevin had done yesterday was a first. It had weighed on him all day and night. Levi wasn't sure he had handled it in the best way that he could have, but he wasn't sure what else he could've done. Thus a sleepless night and a hard jog this morning.

As he reached the back steps of his home, he pulled the towel from the banister where he always left it for when he got back from his run. He dried his face as he stared out across the ocean. He loved Windswept Bay and always had. Loved his job too, but he was starting to feel restless. He'd always put his career first. Always told himself that when he got settled, he would start looking for a wife…but that time had just not come. Instead, he had settled into bachelorhood and unless something major happened, he felt as though he could happily retire as the police chief of Windswept Bay. So what was holding him back from taking the next step in his life?

Nothing except finding the right woman. And why had a little boy and his mother grabbed Levi by the throat and refused to let go? There was obviously something going on there that Levi wasn't sure he wanted to get involved with. And yet the startled expression of Jessica Price when her son had dropped his bomb stuck with Levi. He'd really felt for her.

She'd lost her husband and now her son was struggling. She obviously had a lot on her plate.

He grabbed a bottle of water from the refrigerator as he passed on his way to the shower and glanced at the clock on the wall. He needed to hurry if he was going to make it to the park.

He'd decided it was time to get a dog. Maybe that would help him fill the hole that was suddenly looming in his life. A hole that might have begun while watching his four sisters get married over the last few months. They were happier than he'd ever seen them. Ryan also seemed happier than Levi had ever known him to be.

But Levi was a firm believer that they'd all found happiness when the time had been right. It wasn't as if he was unhappy. And even if he was, he couldn't just go out and find the woman of his dreams just because he decided it was time.

For one, he hadn't decided any such thing. He was just feeling restless.

He took his shower and was dressed and out the front door within thirty minutes. A small puppy to train was just what he needed. The timing was perfect.

A puppy would help.

Jessica watched Kevin and Roscoe run across the large

park area with a couple of the children from the other workers from the shelter. She was so glad to have had this to distract him with today. She'd given everything a long hard look last night and what she came up with was that their situation had been amplified and she had put a lot on him this year by taking this job and moving him away from family and friends.

Making decisions like that lay squarely on her shoulders. It had been less stressful when she could share that burden with Adam. That was one of the things she missed most about Adam: he was so solid, so strong and capable. She sighed. She missed him. Every day, she missed him.

And so why wouldn't it be even harder for Kevin to lose his dad and adjust to his loss?

Watching Kevin laughing and playing did her heart good but it ached. She wanted him to have as normal a life as he could have. And one day she would remarry—if she found a good man who would be wonderful for Kevin.

She'd decided later today she would run by the police station and apologize to Levi again. This time, out of view of the alert six-year-olds.

Her neighbor had agreed to watch Kevin for a few minutes and that was all the time she needed.

His handsome face filled her thoughts as she straightened the clipboards with the waiting forms on them. The college students who were running the event from the shelter were busy talking with potential adoptive doggy parents about certain dogs they were interested in. They were showing each puppy or dog and trying to make the perfect fit. She was in charge of making sure the paperwork was filled out. And this was the best job for her because if she had her way, she would adopt all the dogs and then be unable to feed them or take care of them, and that wouldn't be a good thing.

So she had learned a long time ago that the best thing she could do was to help out the shelter when possible to get the animals adopted by good humans rather than try to save the world.

Two different people were looking at the dogs right now, so she set out two clipboards with the required paperwork just in case they were needed.

When she looked up, she saw a man getting out of a truck in the parking lot. He wore jeans and a dark T-shirt. His dark hair was covered with a ball cap. But even from a hundred yards away, she recognized Levi.

Her stomach dropped and her pulse jumped. How she recognized him from this distance with the ball cap on told her that she had taken notice of him more as a man than she was comfortable admitting. *What was he doing here?*

He entered the fenced area and was halfway to her when he stopped and his gaze locked onto hers. It was more than obvious that he was startled to see her. To his credit, he didn't turn and run but instead continued on to where she stood.

Jessica glanced toward Kevin and prayed he wouldn't look in this direction. And if he did, she prayed harder that the ball cap that Levi wore would conceal his identity from Kevin at this distance. She took a deep breath and forced a smile.

"Police Chief Sinclair, what are you doing here?" She cringed at her greeting. *It wasn't exactly the right way to ask; there had to be a more diplomatic way of—*

"I could ask you the same thing." His gaze flickered to where hers had been moments before and he saw Kevin rolling on the ground with Roscoe.

She looked from Kevin to Levi and their gazes met. He had serious navy eyes and dark lashes she noticed… "I, um, I'm here helping with the adoption program."

"And I just happen to be here to adopt a puppy."

From all accounts, Levi Sinclair was a good guy. Of course, the fact that he was the police chief added to that. It was a very safe community—which was probably a reflection of not only the small community of Windswept Bay but also the fact that he probably did a great job. And that, compounded with the fact he was here to adopt a puppy, made him almost irresistible…If she were interested or thinking about that sort of thing.

"That's wonderful. They brought the dogs that need adopting the most here today. Our goal is not to leave until all ten of them have families, so I really hope you find one you can't live without. But first I really need to apologize to you. I had planned to come by your office this afternoon. Kevin doesn't really understand what he said yesterday." She could not bring herself to repeat the words to him out loud.

"You don't need to keep apologizing. It sounds like Kevin's had a rough go of it. I have broad shoulders and can handle whatever he throws my direction." He gave a smile of encouragement.

"You're sure, Chief Sinclair?"

"Really, it's okay. Don't worry about me. And you can call me Levi. I think yesterday put us on first-name terms, don't you think?"

The man was charming. "I think you're right. I'm Jessica."

"Levi!" A screech of joy pierced the air as Kevin raced toward them.

Panic filled Jessica and she met Levi's gaze.

Levi touched her arm with his fingertips. "It's okay, I understand."

The panic eased slightly. "Thank you," she said just as Kevin came to a halt right in front of Levi.

"I didn't know you were gonna be here. Are you getting a dog?" Kevin cocked his head to the side but kept his bright, star-struck gaze on Levi.

"Is this your dog?" Levi crouched down. He .took the dog's big head between his hands and scratched Roscoe's ears. The dog ate it up like fresh bones; his head lolled to the side and his tongue drooped out.

It was very obvious that Levi knew how to handle dogs. *Did he know how to handle children?*

CHAPTER FOUR

Levi hadn't expected to see Jessica and Kevin here. It seemed that his town had suddenly grown very small. But as he rubbed the huge dog's ears, instead of worrying about what the little kid was going to do next or think or want from him, Levi found his gaze lifting up to meet Jessica's again. The panic he'd seen on Jessica's face had caused his heart to clench and he'd reached out and touched her. He'd wanted to reassure her everything was going to be okay. But was it? Did he know that?

"Are you getting this dog today?" he asked Kevin.

Kevin laughed. "No, Roscoe's already mine. We're just here to help other people adopt dogs. My mom can help you fill out the papers that make a dog yours. She knows exactly what to put on them so that you can take one home with you."

"Oh, so you're saying I can't adopt Roscoe?" Levi teased Kevin and the little boy chuckled.

"No, he's my dog. But I know one you should get."

"Okay, let's do this. Lead the way."

"Come on. I know just the one." Kevin grabbed Levi's hand and pulled him toward the dogs.

Levi glanced at Jessica and saw more worry there. "Are you coming?" he asked. "We might need your help."

She took a deep breath and stepped forward. "Yes, I'm coming."

Kevin led him around the table and into the midst of the dog area. Several men and women who looked like college students were showing dogs to several people. Kevin took Levi past them and past several pens with small dogs in them. He stopped in front of a pen with a large dog sitting inside. It had a big head, massive feet, and the look of a Labrador mixed with something enormous.

"He's a puppy," Kevin declared. "And he's a good'un."

The *puppy* had to weigh forty pounds—and if its feet were any indication, it would weigh a hundred or more pounds before the day was over. Kevin reached in the pen to pet the dog and it nudged its head against Kevin's hand as if seeking his touch.

"I named him Jaco because he just looks like Jaco."

Levi laughed. The little boy was funny. "Well, Jaco fits him perfect." Levi crouched down. "Hey, Jaco. How are you, boy?" The dog slightly cocked his head to look at Levi and Levi knew he'd be leaving here today with this dog. He wondered whether Kevin thought no one would want a big dog or whether he even realized how big the dog would get. But Levi was pretty certain that most people would not want to take such a pup this large home to raise.

"Can we take Jaco out of the pen?" he asked

Jessica. As if understanding what was being said, the dog stood up and put its nose to the fence.

"Yes, certainly. Are you sure?" Jessica asked Levi.

"I'm sure."

"We could put a leash on him and take him out there in the open. Maybe let him run some." Excitement filled Kevin's big eyes.

Levi stood. "Then let's do that." He knew full well that unless something drastic happened and they told him there was no way he could have this dog that he and Jaco were going to grow to be fast buddies.

Moments later, they had Jaco on a leash and the dog was taking them for a walk. The puppy had put his head up in the air and began trying his best to pull them around the park.

Levi laughed and glanced at Kevin. "I think it's obvious that Jaco has been on a leash before. Do you know anything else about his previous owner?"

"I don't know. Do you know, Momma?" Kevin asked as he and Roscoe jogged beside Jaco.

Levi was trying not to focus on the woman beside him. He was trying to focus on the dog and Kevin, but he was very aware of Jessica. He quirked an eyebrow at her.

"I really don't know. I just help out when they have these because they need help. But I agree he's not fighting the leash. He wasn't afraid of it at all. Maybe whoever had him realized he was going to be a giant—maybe they couldn't take care of him and they knew it."

"It makes sense. He's going to be huge." He smiled and she smiled back. They stared at each other for a moment. "So how long have you and Kevin been alone?" he asked, making sure Kevin was busy with the dogs.

"Little over two years. This is our second Christmas without Adam." She glanced at Kevin and then back at him, and there was that pleading in her eyes for understanding. "Which is part of the reason for Kevin's odd actions yesterday. I would like to explain at some point. I'll try now but if he interrupts, I will have to finish later. We moved here because I needed to exert my independence a little bit. I guess most people would think that when you lost someone you loved that having family around and friends and in-laws would be a comfort. And it was, to a point. But I have a very strong-willed family and I felt smothered and…on the spur of the moment, I took this job, after I learned of it through an acquaintance. I didn't ask Kevin. I didn't ask my family. I just accepted it and to everyone's shock, midterm, I loaded up the U-Haul and came cross-country here. It has been a little hard on Kevin—the last two months on top of the whole two years. I don't know what I was thinking. And then this Christmas, I loaded him up for the holidays and took us back to Kansas to see everyone. I think—I don't know—I try to think of all the different reasons but it just boils down to the fact that he missed his dad." She bit her lip and her forehead crinkled as she paused.

"That's understandable."

"Yes, it is. Then, at Christmas, he asked Santa for a daddy and he also prayed to God for a daddy. In his mind he covered all the bases but I didn't know how serious he was until Christmas morning when, all excited, he woke me and dragged me down the stairs to the Christmas tree. Only to find there was no one waiting there. He somehow had literally believed he would have a new daddy there under the tree. Of course there was no daddy under the Christmas tree. I talked with him—my dad talked with him. We thought he understood. You can imagine how startled I was yesterday when he surprised us with his announcement at show-and-tell."

"No more than me." Levi's heart hurt for the little boy. Six years old was a rough time, still believing in the miracle of Christmas and then God's miracles, only to realize that sometimes life is not a fairy tale. "I'm really sorry. It sounds like you had a really rough time."

"It's been hard. We lost Adam quickly and very unexpectedly. He was a hero—he rescued a family from their car during a flood and after he got them out, he didn't make it out. He was strong and he would want me to be strong. It's been tough and not having anyone to discuss things with has been really hard."

He could tell she was a strong woman; he admired that about her. "What about your family?"

"Like I said, they're very strong-willed. I talked to them about some things but there's a point of understanding and a point of overtaking, and I need to be my own boss. And so I'm here." She bit her lip again. "Enough about me. I'm excited and so is Kevin that you're going to adopt Jaco. Aren't you?"

He laughed. "Yes, how can I resist?"

She laughed. "I totally understand. He's big but adorable."

Kevin raced up; the kid raced everywhere.

"So what do you think? Should I adopt Jaco?" Levi bent down and rubbed Jaco's head and immediately Roscoe put his big head between the two of them. Levi laughed. "I think I've created a monster where Roscoe is concerned."

Kevin nodded. "Yes," he said. "Jaco wants to be with you. And we can come to your house or come to the park and let Roscoe and Jaco play."

It hit Levi then that he'd just been set up by a six-year-old again. A barely four feet tall six year old who looked more like a hopeful preschooler. But looking up at Jessica, Levi suddenly realized he didn't mind so much. He actually didn't mind at all.

"I think that's a great idea," he said.

Instantly Kevin reacted with glee as he looked up at his mom. She gave Kevin a tight smile that didn't reach her eyes as her gaze met Levi's.

"Kevin, you and Roscoe play here, and I'll take Levi to fill out paperwork."

"But I want to come," Kevin argued.

"No, you stay here. He can see you before he leaves."

Levi heard the warning in her words and knew that Kevin understood she meant what she said. She looked at him. "Come with me."

What had he done? He watched her walk away. Because clearly he had done something.

"I'll bring Jaco over here when I get through." He told Kevin and then he went to catch up with Jessica. She had paused a few feet away to wait for him and as he drew close to her, he saw anger in her expression.

"What are you doing?" She hissed marching farther away from Kevin. "I know that you don't completely understand what you're doing, but telling him you're going to start meeting him with the dog and playing in the park, or-or," she stammered, "having us come over for him to play with the dog at your house is not what Kevin needs right now. He just introduced an entire classroom to you as his daddy-to-be. This is not helping. I explained things to him. I told him you are not going to be his daddy and what he did was wrong. So your encouraging him like this isn't helping. He has a heart you know. And the last thing he needs is for you to get his hopes up for something that isn't happening. What were you thinking?"

Levi watched her spin away and start walking, he'd messed up alright. And she was right, what had he been thinking?

Jessica was fuming. She told herself that Levi didn't understand what he was doing. This was her son and she was already in over her head on how to handle what was going on. She had seen the joy in Kevin's expression when he realized that Levi had said they would play with the dogs in the park together. She closed her eyes; it was just too much to think about.

Suddenly, she tripped—walking with her eyes closed was also not good. Her eyes flew open immediately. She would have hit the ground but Levi's strong arms wrapped around her and saved her. Her pulse went crazy as he held her close and she found herself looking up at him.

"Are you okay?"

She nodded and pushed away. "I'm fine." She lied, nothing about her was okay right now.

"Look, I didn't mean any harm with Kevin. I thought I was helping. I wouldn't do anything to hurt him or any child."

Her pulse had not calmed down. It raced erratically through her veins as she tried to hold his gaze. "I believe that. I just don't think you understand the consequences of our situation right now." She had enough to worry about without Kevin getting his hopes up by spending time with Levi. If ever there was anyone to have some distance from, it was him.

She grabbed one of the clipboards and held it out to him. "Take that pen attached to that clipboard and fill this out, and then you will be able to take Jaco home with you."

Levi took the clipboard but didn't take his eyes off her. They were troubled...and beautiful with their midnight depths looking almost iridescent in the sunlight. She crossed her arms, trying not to let the moment make her feel bad about being upset. This was about Kevin.

"I understand what you're saying. I hear you loud and clear. And I get it." He gave her a look of kindness before he began to fill out the paperwork. That kindness only made this harder because she liked him. He was a really nice man.

And...there was something about him that-she stopped herself right then, not willing to explore anything else about Levi Sinclair that distracted her from the problem at hand.

Hours later, Levi found himself at the grocery store, looking for a different kind of dog food than the dog food he'd picked up on the way home from the park.

Jaco refused to eat that food—he basically refused to do anything except sit by the window and stare out of it.

It was as though he thought he was still in his kennel and that the glass window was his view out. So Levi had come to the store to find something else to entice the dog to eat. He hoped tomorrow would be better. Of course it would take time for the dog to acclimate to his new surroundings. He expected that. But he felt for the poor animal.

Levi was in the dog food aisle when he heard his name being called. He turned to see a woman and a little girl a few feet from him.

"There he is, Mommy. He's going to be Kevin's new daddy."

What? Then he recognized the little girl as the girl with the mother who said he was a hunk—among other things.

The mother looked at him with dark-blue, curious eyes. "My Lisa told me you were getting married. That's too sad," she said in a voice full of regret.

"No, I'm not getting married." He reacted

instantly.

Her expression brightened. "Oh really? Then you're still on the market?"

"No. I mean, yes. But—"

She took a step closer. "I've admired you for a long time." She let her gaze move over him and her eyes twinkled as they came back to his. "I would love to have dinner with you…I would even cook dinner for you—"

He stepped back. "I'm sorry. I'm pretty busy right now. But," he backed up another step and grabbed the bag of dog food he'd been eyeing, "thank you for the offer." *What else was he supposed to say?*

She placed a hand on his arm. "The offer stands. Anytime. My name's Trisha Mosley. Call me."

Levi looked from her to her little girl and he smiled, not sure how to react.

The six-year-old glared at him. "You lied. Why did you say you were going to be Kevin's daddy?"

"I didn't say—" He stopped himself from explaining himself to a six-year-old. "I need to go. My dog is waiting on food." And with that, he turned and strode away and turned the corner the minute he reached it. *This was ridiculous.* He was the chief of police and he was running…from a six-year-old and her mom.

He paid for the dog food and forced himself not to look over his shoulder. He was halfway to his car when he realized that if it had been Jessica Price who had been in that dog food aisle giving him an open invitation to dinner, he would have jumped at the chance in a heartbeat.

But after today, he knew there'd be a snowstorm on the Florida coast before that would happen.

He thought about Jessica and Kevin all the way back home. When he walked into the kitchen, he was startled to find Jaco waiting at the door. "Well, hey there, Jaco." His heart warmed at the idea that the pup might actually be glad to see him.

Jaco tilted his big brown head to the side and studied him as his tail did a halfhearted tap against the floor.

"It's okay, buddy. You can relax because you're here to stay. I've already reconciled myself to the fact that you're going to be as big as a small cow. It's okay." He patted Jaco's head and set the bag of dog food on the floor. "Now, let's see if you'll eat this brand. Because I don't know if you realize it but a growing dog like yourself needs to eat."

Levi opened the bag and poured some in the large pan that he was using for a dog bowl. And immediately, Jaco started to eat.

Relieved that at least that had been accomplished, Levi raked his hand through his hair and leaned against the counter to watch his dog eat.

His phone rang and he answered it.

"Hey, man." It was his brother Jake. "Have you been holding out on us? I heard from a client at the dive shop today that you're getting married?"

Levi rubbed the back of his neck. "No, it's not true. But I have a feeling everyone in town is going to think so before long."

And Jessica had probably realized this was going to happen. That was why she'd apologized again. He quickly told Jake what had happened at the show-and-tell and what had just happened today, including the grocery store incident.

Jake let out a low whistle. "That's wild. So at least you know you can and should get a date. Maybe this is your sign that there's more to life than work."

Levi glanced at Jaco. The dog was watching him. "Yeah, you might have a point. Same goes for you, though," he said with a short laugh. "I haven't seen you looking to settle down."

"I may not be adverse to the situation. I am at least dating. I'm looking for *love*." He drew out the word *love* in a long, slow exaggeration.

"That you are doing, there is no denying that. Okay, I got to go take my dog for a walk."

"Sounds good. Maybe you should go to the dog park—probably a lot of single dog owners there. Maybe even a cute teacher." Jake ended with a chuckle as the phone line went dead.

Levi thought of Jessica and wondered whether she just might be at the dog park. He looked at Jaco. "What do you think about going to the dog park?"

The dog barked instantly, as if it knew exactly what Levi was talking about.

CHAPTER FIVE

If Jessica had to tell one other person that she was not getting married anytime soon—and especially to the chief of police—she would scream. What had she been thinking when she woke that morning and decided to take Kevin to church? After what happened on Friday, she should have known this was a bad idea. The questions started immediately. The first person she met asked the question and by the time the sixth person had asked the same question, she was ready to grab her purse and her child and get out of there.

Of course she hadn't but all through the service,

she felt as if she had eyeballs glued to her back because as odd as it was, several women in the congregation were not happy at the idea of the handsome police chief getting married. Hopefully, after repeating herself several times, those women would hear the truth and realize that the chief was still available and it had only been a rumor started by her confused child.

Jillian Locke, her new friend, who just happened to be Levi's sister, caught up to her after the service and grinned mischievously. "So I hear we're going to be sisters-in-law. You should have told me." Her eyes twinkled.

"Oh Jillian, what am I going to do? These people around here obviously think your brother is the cat's meow and are not happy with even the remote idea that he is off the market. Even if it's not true. I felt daggers in my back through the whole church service." She leaned close. "Don't you feel them?" She hitched her head slightly to the right and Jillian's eyes followed the direction that Jessica indicated.

Two women stood across the lawn in deep

conversation as they stared toward Jessica.

"Oh, you're talking about Loretta and Diane. Those two have been chasing my poor brother since high school. I can tell you right now that you don't have any competition from them."

Jessica looked at Jillian in disbelief. "No, they have no competition from me. Your brother and I barely know each other. He simply came to the show-and-tell because you and Ryan took Kevin to the station and I guess introduced them. The poor guy was blindsided by my son. I was too."

"So maybe that was a sign or something. My brother is a great guy who works too much and doesn't think enough of his own needs right now. He's given everything he's got to this town since becoming police chief. And just between you and me, he's getting a little set in his ways and it's time for him to settle down. Olivia, Cali, and Shar agree."

"But I don't. I'm not ready for a step like that."

Jillian stared at her with compassion. "Believe me when I tell you that I understand not being ready for a new chapter in your life. Before Christmas, I learned that there's a very good possibility that I may not be able to have children and I want children so bad. I want to know what it's like to carry my child, my own baby. But that may not happen."

Jessica couldn't believe it. "I am so sorry," she said.

"Thank you but I'm telling you this to let you know that I wasn't ready to learn that when I did. And then Ryan walked back into my life and believe me when I tell you we are trying to see if there is a possibility of me carrying our child. But if I don't conceive over the next year or so, then we will move onto other options. I'm just telling you this even though you losing your husband and me having my situation—they don't compare apples to apples, but the ordeal that I went through before Ryan and I found each other again is similar. You cope and you move on with your life. When the time is right. That may not make any sense but let's just say don't shut your door to possibilities. Leave the light on and see what happens."

Jessica thought about that all the way home. She

had felt like the light had been turned off when Adam died and she wasn't sure she could turn that light back on just yet.

But obviously Kevin was ready to flip the switch.

They were passing the dog park on the way to the house when Kevin began to bounce in the backseat. She glanced at him in the rearview. "What has got you so excited?"

"Can we take Roscoe to the dog park? He really liked it yesterday."

"No, you can play with Roscoe in the backyard."

"Aw, Momma, he can run and play in the big area and he only has that small backyard. He's a big dog. His legs get cramped. And, and…he, he needs some playtime."

She glanced back at Kevin again and decided that today maybe they all needed to go to the dog park. She didn't have the energy to be mom-the-fun-buster today. "Okay, it's a beautiful day for the dog park."

Kevin whooped with happiness and barely gave her time to change into jeans and a light sweatshirt when they got back to the house. There was a slight breeze today; the January temperatures were lower than the normal warm temperature that Windswept Bay had most of the year. But it didn't take them long to get Roscoe loaded into the vehicle, along with her hyper child.

When they got to the park, there were just three other vehicles there. She didn't really pay them much attention as she parked beside a truck and they got out. Roscoe and Kevin raced through the gate and into the park area ahead of her. It wasn't until she made it through and was latching the gate that she saw where her son and his dog were headed. Straight to the familiar form of Levi Sinclair. And Jaco.

They stood in the center of the park. Levi held a stick, probably teaching Jaco to play fetch. Jessica groaned even as excitement filled her. It was confusing to say the least.

He saw her and to her surprise, he smiled with genuine pleasure, even after she'd jumped all over him hard the day before.

"Hi, Levi. Are you teaching him to fetch?" Kevin asked. "Roscoe knows how to fetch. Throw the stick for him and he can teach Jaco." Kevin rattled his sentences off in rapid-fire.

Levi threw the stick. That's all it took for Roscoe to bound into action as he raced after the stick and Jaco followed. So did Kevin.

"We need to stop meeting like this," Levi said.

There was a distinct sexiness in his voice that sent a shiver through Jessica.

She wasn't ready for this, she told herself firmly, as something inside her seemed to un-curl just a little. "I'm truly not stalking you."

"I know that. Yesterday you were here first. And I am the one who showed up."

"Oh, that's right. So how are you and Jaco getting along?" Focusing on the dog was a safe area of conversation.

"I'm not sure yet. He's not eating real well. I switched foods twice and the second one, he ate a little bit this morning but he's not eating like I think you should be eating for a dog his size."

"He's probably just getting acclimated. What are you feeding him?" She watched the two dogs and her son race after the stick that Kevin had picked up and thrown again.

Levi told her the name of the two different foods that he was feeding Jaco.

"Jaco is almost old enough to eat regular food. I could give you some that we feed Roscoe and you can try that. Roscoe seems to like it a lot." She wondered what she was doing because him getting the dog food from her would mean he would have to come to her house. But that would be fine.

"Are you sure? I wouldn't want to impose but if you think there's a chance that Jaco would eat it then I'll take you up on that offer. I'm worried about him."

"Then after they play here at the park, you can follow me to the house and I will get you some. We had to get it at the veterinarian's office and they're closed today or I would send you there."

"I'd appreciate that. Other than the food situation, I think he and I will get along. But I am glad that you showed up. He really likes playing with Roscoe and Kevin. We've been here for about an hour and he hasn't shown this much excitement the whole time."

Jessica's gaze narrowed. "You've been here for an hour?" She thought back to when Kevin had asked to come to the dog park. She glanced at the parking lot, noting that Levi's truck was very visible from the road as they would've passed. *She had been set up.*

"Yeah, been here for an hour. Why?"

"Nothing. I just—" She paused and decided not to tell him that they had been set up. "Was wondering."

They started walking now. Levi had to jump out of the way when Kevin raced past, laughing, while both dogs were on his heels. She laughed and felt happiness tumble through her at the sound of Kevin's joy.

"Have you felt any repercussions from show-and-tell yet?" Levi arched a brow as he slid a glance her way.

"Do you mean things like daggers in my back from females who have heard that the police chief is getting married? If that's what you're asking, then yes, I have." She laughed. "Did you know that you are a very popular guy in Windswept Bay?" She smiled at him, unable to help herself, especially when he grimaced.

"Yeah, I had an incident myself. Plus it was a little embarrassing in class that day at what the kids were saying." He shook his head. "I've been working a lot. I didn't really think about it that much. Until lately—as in Friday." He laughed and looked slightly embarrassed.

She liked that about him. It was almost as if he didn't understand or realize why single women would be upset that a guy like him was getting married—or that they *thought* he was getting married, she reminded herself.

The having to remind herself of such a thing was a little bit disconcerting.

"So you don't date?" *Why was she asking such a personal question?*

"Not much. It's been a little while since I had a date—several months at least."

She shrugged. "It's been awhile since I had a date too." She cleared her throat. "But you know I've had my reasons for that. And you may have too. I don't really know you but you seem like a guy with a great career, well thought of from all who know you and as far as I know, nothing getting in your way."

She had no idea why she was talking about this with him other than the fact that it was just nice to be talking to someone…a man. She had conversations with women all the time but other than the few men who taught at her school, it had been a long time since she'd really had a conversation and it felt good. Even if her curiosity was getting in the way.

He looked straight at her. His gaze turned serious, as if she'd just been caught speeding far over the speed limit. It was unsettling.

"I meet women around town all the time…but until now, I haven't felt the need to pursue anyone."

Jessica's pulse pounded, as if she'd just driven over a cliff and her foot was heavy on the gas pedal. She took a step back and glanced toward Kevin and the dogs. "I think we should go play with the dogs and Kevin." She didn't wait for him to agree but instead started walking toward her laughing son. She needed something to redirect the conversation because she was almost certain that Levi had just told her he was interested in her. *And that was not good. Was it? No—it wasn't*, she told herself firmly.

But she had a problem as she walked. She knew that something had just stirred inside her. Something she hadn't felt for a very long time: *interest*.

There was something here, between her and this man. And Jessica didn't know how to feel about that.

"Momma, watch Jaco get the stick. Roscoe taught him." Kevin threw the stick as hard as his little six-year-old arms could throw it. The dogs thundered after it and Kevin turned, laughing, to look at her.

Kevin's face beamed with excitement, more excitement than Jessica had seen in ages. They were treading on dangerous waters. "That's wonderful." She struggled to maintain eye contact with him and not to glance at Levi, who had come to stand beside her.

"How did you teach them to do that so fast?" Levi asked.

Kevin shrugged. "It's easy. I just played with them."

Levi laughed. "Easy for you, kiddo. That's amazing. I obviously have a long way to go. I think you must be a dog whisperer or something, kid." As if truly stunned by what Kevin had accomplished in just a short few minutes, Levi shot a perplexed glance at Jessica. "I can't get my dog to eat and Kevin has taught him to fetch in under twenty minutes. How?"

Jessica could not help but chuckle. Levi wasn't kidding. And it was kind of amazing but then Kevin did have a way with dogs, just like his dad had. "He is kind of a dog whisperer, just so you know. Adam was a service dog trainer. He had a way with animals. And though Kevin was only four when his dad died, Kevin had spent most of his life traveling behind his dad as Adam worked with service dogs in our kennel. He had his dad's gift early on and it was apparent. Dogs respond to him."

Kevin beamed again. "My daddy taught dogs how to do all kinds of cool stuff. There was a man who had—" Kevin paused, deep in thought. "DTEP. He had DTSP and he had nightmares and he shook a lot sometimes. My dad taught his dog to help him. And the man was all better when his dog would put his head on his knee."

"The man had PTSD, Post-Traumatic Stress

Disorder?" Levi asked.

"Yes, that's it. I never get it right." Kevin looked seriously at Levi. "It came from the war."

"That's okay," Levi said, with compassion in his voice. "I think that's really awesome that your daddy helped men who were in the war."

"Me too. If he hadn't died, he would help more. My daddy was like you," Kevin said, staring earnestly up at Levi. "Police officers help people. My daddy helped people. And I'm going to help people too."

Jessica's heart caught. She swallowed hard as she looked from her son to Levi.

Levi's gaze touched hers briefly before he focused back on Kevin. "I'm sure your daddy would like knowing you're following in his footsteps."

"I can't follow his footsteps because he's not here now," Kevin said solemnly. "But I can follow yours." He smiled. And then spinning away, he ran to the dogs and hugged both of them. Then he picked up the stick and threw it again.

Jessica watched him and she felt Levi beside her doing the same. They watched him in silence for a few moments.

"Are you okay?" Levi asked at last.

"As good as I can be," she said, hearing the thickness in her voice. "My son has a good heart."

"It sounds like he gets that from you and his father."

She looked at him then and felt understanding pass between them. "I like to think so. Adam was the best man I ever knew." Her voice cracked. "I don't think I'm as good a person as he was a man."

"And why do you say that?" Levi asked, disbelief in his tone.

She sniffed. "Because I have to fight being really angry that he died saving someone, and left his own son here to grow up without him."

She felt horrible saying such a thing but in moments like this, she felt as though her baby needed his daddy so badly. Now Levi knew what a horrible person she was. But maybe that was a good thing. If he realized she wasn't as good a person as he obviously thought she was, then maybe he would walk away.

And that would be for the best.

CHAPTER SIX

Levi felt an overwhelming need to pull Jessica into his arms and hold her tight, to plant a gentle kiss against her temple and to smooth her hair away from her face so he could try to ease the tension and pain she felt. His heart was touched by these two. And by the man who had died saving another family and in the process left his family behind.

"I think those are probably normal feelings, don't you?"

She looked away. "Maybe. But I still have them and if it had been me who died, Adam would have probably just been so proud of me for saving lives that he might not have such thoughts."

Unable to stop himself, he took her arm and gently turned her back so that she faced him. "I think you're wrong about that. If he's as good a man as you say and if he loved you as much as I'm sure he did, then he would have hated losing you, no matter what the circumstances were. Those thoughts of yours are wrong. I barely know you and I know this." He'd known her for three days and known Kevin for four days. But he knew if something were to happen to them tomorrow, he would never forget them. "I know your husband would have been devastated, absolutely no question about it, if he had lost you. Or Kevin."

She took a deep breath. "Thank you. What must you think of us? It seems that it might appear that my life is falling apart instead of me getting it back together again."

"Not at all. I've seen a lot of loss in my business. Loss, I think, comes in ebbs and flows like the tide. And eventually the tide goes out and it just gently laps back in, but it's never completely gone and I don't think anyone wants it to be. My grandma told me after my grandpa died when I was worrying about her because she was crying one day that as his grandson, I missed him terribly but as his wife of sixty years, she missed him more. I understood that even though I was young and she said that her tears had eased but would always come, at least she hoped so, because they meant that my granddaddy had lived and been loved. There's nothing wrong with that. Didn't mean she was moving on."

Jessica took a deep breath and slowly let it out. He could tell she was taking it all in.

"Thank you. I think I understand completely why I received daggers in my back at church this morning and why my classroom reacted so adamantly about how their mothers felt when Kevin started the rumor that you were getting married. It's not hard to tell that you are a great guy. And you are really holding someone's happiness at bay every day that you aren't looking for her."

He grinned. "All I can say is until the time is right, I'm not forcing the issue. Have you and Kevin eaten lunch?"

She probably would say no but he asked anyway. The thought of her leaving and going a different direction than him right now was just not something he wanted. He didn't look any further other than the fact that he wanted to spend more time with her and he wanted her to be his friend. He had a feeling that's all she had room in her life for right now and that was fine with him. For now.

"I should say no." She held his gaze. "But lunch sounds good. Though it can be touchy where Kevin is concerned."

"I understand that. I also understand that you living your life avoiding friendships or holding yourself back from people could be hard. So I'll be careful."

"Then lunch sounds fine."

"Hey, Kevin, are you hungry?"

"Yes," the kid yelled and raced back in their direction, with the dogs trailing. "Can we have pizza? I'm really hungry for pizza."

"You're always hungry for pizza. You're going to

turn into a pepperoni."

Levi laughed. "It's a coincidence but I am starving for pizza too."

Jessica rolled her eyes. "Then I guess pizza it is."

"Then let's load up and go grab that pizza."

He had a feeling this could be messy but right now the day seemed bright and shining.

Lana was waiting in the drop-off lane. It was their morning to work the student drop-off as mothers drove into the school and let the kids out for the day. Her face was bright with open curiosity as Jessica met her on the sidewalk.

"So I heard at the teacher lounge this morning that you were spotted at the pizzeria on Main with none other than Kevin's future daddy." She chuckled and then her eyes narrowed. "What is going on?"

"I have no idea, Lana. I think I have lost my blooming mind. You cannot believe everything that happened this weekend." She told her quickly about meeting Levi at the dog park for the adoption and then

Sunday morning at church and then her son setting them up in the dog park to play after he had seen Levi's truck there on the way home from church. And then her conversation with Levi and that she accepted a lunch date that really wasn't a date…it was just lunch. Period.

And it had been wonderful. But she wasn't telling Lana that.

Cars pulled up and they had to unload kids but the moment there was an opening, Lana came back over.

"Sooo," she cooed, coming back to stand beside Jessica. "This has been a very eventful three days. But I'm curious about the lunch date with the sexy police chief. How'd that go?" She drawled slowly and waggled her brows.

Jessica sighed. "Oh Lana, he's really wonderful." And he was…which was the problem. "I understand why so many women seem to be upset by rumors that he might be off the market…no matter how untrue the rumors are."

"You like him." She gasped. "Oh, Jessica, that's wonderful. It sounds like you've connected."

"But, it's not that simpl—"

Her friend grabbed her by the arms. "Don't shut the door on this. Take a deep breath and take it slow. It's been two years since you lost Adam, and I know there are things going on in your head and heart that only someone who has lost a husband or a wife would understand. But, I do understand that there was something sparkling in your eyes for just a moment and I saw it."

"No—"

Lana smiled. "There is something going on here. Don't just shut it down."

"I'm scared, Lana. And just that alone makes me feel guilty."

"I get that. And I bet it's going to be a process that will sort itself out. As long as you don't shut down. Promise me you won't slam the door on at least exploring this new possibility."

Jessica's stomach felt shaky but she nodded. "Okay. I'm not promising anything is going to happen but I'll try to not run away from the process."

Lana's eyes softened. "Good for you. I'm here,

you know. Anytime you need me."

"Thanks. You have no idea how comforting that is." It was huge.

On Monday afternoon, Max, Levi's brother who was special ops with the military, stopped by the office. He walked in holding a cake wrapped in decorative cellophane and frilly curly ribbons.

Levi had just come in from a zoning meeting in which he had been asked by several people whether the rumors were true that he was getting married.

"Special delivery." Max held the cake out to him.

Max was leaving on an assignment, and as it always was, no one knew where he was going or when he'd be back.

"So I can tell you're about to leave town but I'm not sure why you're bringing me a cake. I should be sending you off with one."

"I didn't bring this to you. It was sitting outside on the sidewalk and it's got your name on it with the card." He grinned and set the cake on the desk.

Levi took the cake and glanced at the card. Sure enough, scrawled in pretty handwriting was his name. He looked inside and read. *The invitation still stands.*

His thoughts went to the woman at the grocery store and her dinner invitation.

"So is it true you have rumors rampaging about you and secret admirers all over the place? And now you're getting cakes dropped off at the doorstep of the police station...interesting, brother." Max didn't try to hide the humor he was feeling for the situation.

"It's true," Betty Lou called from the dispatch room. "Your brother is now the most wanted man in town." Betty Lou's chuckles spilled from the small dispatch room and flowed into their area.

"Betty Lou, I told you this morning, it's not funny anymore."

"From where I see it, it's hilarious," she called back.

Levi shook his head and met his brother's laughing eyes.

Max cocked his head to one side. "Betty Lou, I tend to be with you on this one. Chief, you going to be married by the time I get back?"

"Don't egg her on, Max. All this will pass over by the time you get back, unless you're leaving today and come back tomorrow. But your missions usually take at least a week, so I'm hoping that in a week it's all gone."

"I'll probably be back by the end of the week. I'm not sure what we're doing but I have a feeling it's probably a three-day mission. That's all I can say, but you know the rules. Anyway, I want to come by and ask if you'll check on my place a few times and feed the animals."

"You got it. Stay safe out there." Levi held his hand out.

Max grabbed the firm shake and then they hugged.

"I'm always careful."

"I hear you, but it doesn't hurt to say the words. Keep low and don't get cocky."

Max grinned. "Seems you need to take care of your own self while I'm gone. That cake looks like serious business. You may have a whole bakery piled up out there soon."

Levi paused, considering the worrisome suggestion. "Nah, not happening." At least he hoped not. He was here to protect the people of Windswept Bay, not be the focus of a husband hunt.

Max put his hands on his hips and studied him. "In all those Hallmark movies our sisters watched growing up, I think things like that happen all the time. I'd watch out for cakes."

"I'll send them your way," Levi grunted. They walked out of the office and onto the sidewalk. He had no idea where these rumors were heading but he knew that the only person he'd like to get a cake from was Jessica and he wasn't sure what to do about that. He had to get her off his mind. "You'll be home in time for Mom's birthday then?"

"I hope so. It'll be a nice birthday bash," Max said.

"I think Cam is coming down too, even though he was just here for Christmas. He's spending more time down here lately and I'm starting to wonder if he's missing his roots."

"I noticed that too. I'm glad he'll be here because

if somehow I don't make it back in time, well, at least everyone else will be." He glanced at his watch. "Okay, I got to be at the base soon. And hey." He looked over his shoulder as he put his hand on the door handle of his truck. "If something happens and by the time I get back you do happen to be hitched or nearly hitched, more power to you, man."

"Not happening." Levi laughed. "But to be honest, I do like Jessica. But she's lost her first husband and she has a very tender, fragile heart right now. There's not much room for more than just getting to know her better for the time being."

"I like that you are interested in someone. It's time because you're settled. Me, I'm not settling down, not with my erratic schedule and the risk involved. Oh, hey, I hear you got a new pup."

Levi laughed. "You should see my pup. He's so big. I knew nobody was going to adopt that dog and I couldn't resist him."

"Love at first sight. I hear it happens between a man and a woman too." Max grinned. "Gotta go."

"We'll leave a light on for you. See you soon."

Max climbed into his truck, gave a quick wave and then headed out. Levi was proud of his brother and the country should be too.

Instead of going back inside, he decided to take a walk down to the boat dock. Ryan was making the rounds and so was his other deputy. A little fresh air would do him good right now. He didn't tell Max but he hadn't slept a lot last night and had a certain strawberry-blonde on his mind.

She'd been on his mind ever since he'd first met her. And he had a feeling it was going to be that way for a very long time.

CHAPTER SEVEN

On Wednesday, Jessica dropped Kevin off at her friend's house for a play date, and had three hours all to herself. As a single parent and his schoolteacher, three hours alone was not something to be wasted. She contemplated treating herself to a rare manicure and a pedicure but then she thought about lunch with Jillian. They'd been trying to do lunch for a while now and not getting a time worked out.

She dialed the number. "Hey, Jillian, it's Jessica."

"Jessica, it is so good to hear from you."

She sounded as if she were rushing, maybe

walking really fast. "You sound busy. I was calling about maybe having coffee since we haven't found time for lunch. I find myself with a few free hours today."

"Oh, that would be so great. But I can't. I'm actually about to walk into the doctor's office for an appointment right now. We are having the worst time getting our schedules to match up. But maybe tomorrow?"

"We'll get it worked out. Is everything okay? You're not sick, I hope."

There was a pause. "No, the truth is I'm seeing the doctor to find out if I'm expecting. Don't say anything to anyone please because the odds are against me but I have to tell you I'm nervous right now. "Don't be. Wish me luck—better yet, say a prayer for me and Ryan."

"Oh, you bet," Jessica said, understanding how important this moment was for them.

"Okay, I've got to go, but we will do lunch or coffee soon."

After ending the call, Jessica said a prayer for her

friend and then decided coffee on her own would have to do. She'd grab her favorite mocha latte and a piece of cheesecake and just chill for thirty minutes as she decided what to do with her other two hours.

She parked her car at the local coffee shop and entered the building. It was a busy place and she had to wait in line. The door opened behind her and she turned to see Levi walk in. Her breath caught and her pulse instantly jumped.

Her conversation with Lana rang in her ears as his gaze met hers and he crossed the room to come to stand behind her.

"We are going to have to stop meeting like this." He had a smile in his voice and an enticing twinkle in his eyes.

He looked so good and there was no denying that she was happy to see him. "We are definitely working with similar mindsets lately."

He chuckled. "I'm not complaining at all. How are you?"

He looked as if he was happy to see her. Her stomach felt bottomless and she had to admit that she was glad to see him. "I'm good," she said with a little hesitancy.

"If you're here alone, I'd love to join you."

How could she resist him? "Sure. I had a few spare hours while Kevin is at a friend's house. They are working on a project. I don't think it's fair of me to be helping him with his project when I'm the teacher, so he goes to his friend's house and they work on it together. And it gives him a chance to be with someone other than me all the time."

It was her time to order, so she asked for coffee and cheesecake.

He grinned. "I came to get my coffee at the perfect time today. I'll have the same thing she's having and I'll take the check please," he said to the girl.

"Sure, Chief," the girl said. "I heard you were getting married."

He glanced at Jessica, and she forced her expression to remain neutral.

"Sandy, it's just a rumor."

"So my sister still stands a chance?" Sandy smiled teasingly and Jessica got the feeling the high-school-aged girl was just teasing him.

"Melinda will always own my heart."

"She will be so happy."

They moved to the end of the counter to wait on their order and Jessica couldn't help asking, "So you and Melinda?"

"Yup. She's a great little gal. I'll be getting married in about eighteen years or so. Melinda is four."

Jessica laughed. "Oh, so now I understand."

"I have a feeling she'll lose interest before the wedding date and leave me broken-hearted."

"Let's hope so anyway." She liked him more and more. And he was so good with kids, it was obvious…or at least he was when he wasn't being ambushed in a roomful of them. "So, you're off again today?"

"Imagine that, the police chief gets time off."

"Imagine." Her smile widened.

"I'm about to drive out to my brother Max's place and check on it for him since he had to go out of town yesterday. But I can do that after cheesecake."

Their order came up and they went to a table by

the window. "So, Max is your brother who is in the military?" she said with a little uncertainty. She and Jillian had talked a little bit and she knew some about his family. But there were so many of them, Jessica was almost guessing.

She knew he had four brothers and four sisters and therefore with nine of them, getting all their names straight was a task in itself.

"Yeah, Max is in special ops with the SEALs. He's on a mission. And when he's on a mission, I go by and check on his place every couple of days. It's several miles outside of town."

"That's nice of you. So he's on a mission? A dangerous mission?"

"I'm sure if he's been called out, then it's very dangerous. Missions that nobody will ever know about."

"I don't know if I could deal with that. If I was married to a man who was in such a dangerous career, I would be worried all the time. Life is dangerous enough already. Your job is too dangerous for me."

"My job isn't going straight into combat situations

like Max. There are risks just walking out of your house and getting into your car every day. You can't live your life being afraid. Prepared, but not afraid."

She knew he was probably right but she also knew that he was minimizing the danger for her benefit. "I tend to worry more than I should."

"I would think after losing your husband like you did, in such a traumatic way, that you would worry more."

She sipped her coffee, thinking about how much she should share. He was going to think that all she talked about was Adam's death. But he seemed interested. "Right after he died, I had this calm come over me. Like I understood that everything happens for a reason and that everything about your life is set in stone and when it is your time to go, you'll go." She paused, remembering those horrible first hours and days after Adam died. "As odd as it sounds, I felt peace about that and I was ready to go. It was as if I had one foot in the door of heaven, with Adam already there." She wondered what Levi would say to that.

His expression tightened. "I hate that you went

through that. Do you feel that way now?"

She shrugged. "Time heals. It doesn't make me forget, but it helps me feel more like my old self. And I don't know if I'll ever marry again, but I do know it wouldn't be to someone who has a risky job. I've lost too much and don't want to go through that again if I can help it."

Levi looked thoughtful and then he took a drink of his coffee before he put a fork in his cheesecake. She did the same.

"So," he said at last. "Hypothetically speaking, you're saying someone like me would never have a chance with you."

She cringed. "I didn't mean it like that. I…you're a great guy, but I don't think so. I…don't think I would let myself fall for you or someone like you or like your brother."

He had placed his hand on the table beside his coffee and now his long fingers tapped silently on the table as if counting the beats while he thought. After a moment, his gaze dug into hers. "I don't think I'm going to like that. But I'll take my chances because I really like being your friend."

She was having a hard time concentrating on anything but the look in his eyes: intense and totally focused. She was mesmerized by him. And she didn't know what to say… *Ha*—she didn't know what to think.

His lips quirked upward. "Stop worrying. I see it in your eyes. I get it. All of it." He held his hand out to her. "Friends?"

She stared at that hand. And she was almost afraid to take it. Afraid of the sparks that she knew his touch ignited in her. But she had promised Lana that she wouldn't run. "Friends."

The moment she placed her hand in his, and the rougher, manly feel of his grasp met her softer skin, her stomach dropped to her toes.

"Good. I'm glad we're friends at least. Going to Max's will take me about an hour round trip. Would you like to ride out with me? He lives in a unique place—it's worth the drive. No strings attached."

She had started to sip her coffee and stopped. "I don't know." She knew she shouldn't say yes. That she should go home and do laundry or something else just that exciting before picking Kevin up in a little over two hours. But, well, this was an opportunity to do something...something for herself. She felt guilty even for contemplating it but she nodded anyway. "Okay," she said and she could hear Lana applauding her.

She decided that Lana might be a bad influence.

Levi's smile of genuine pleasure caused butterflies to erupt behind her ribs.

"Great." He paused as they both stared at each other, as if not sure where to go from that moment. He chuckled, easing the sudden tension between them. "Then finish off that cheesecake. You've barely started and it's too good to leave behind. As you can see, I'm going to finish off my last two bites. We'll head out when you're done." He dug his fork into his dessert.

Suddenly feeling lighthearted, she cut into her cheesecake and took a bite. It melted against her tongue but she barely tasted it now.

Moments later, they were loaded in his truck and headed out of town. Her stomach alternated between feeling bottomless and churning with nervous energy.

She tried to ignore both and pretend that it had nothing to do with her attraction for the appealing man driving the truck.

No, these feelings were merely excitement at doing something spontaneous, having some fun. Of getting out of the house for some free time. That was it, she assured herself.

It had nothing to do with attraction.

Nothing at all.

CHAPTER EIGHT

"So do you enjoy teaching?" Levi asked a few miles down the road. He'd been thinking about what she'd said back at the coffee shop. The loss of her husband and how it had affected her. How she'd felt as though she already had one foot in heaven's door. And then about his job being too dangerous. She seemed just as lost in thought as he was since they'd gotten into his truck.

"I do enjoy it," she said. "And I love having a couple of months off in the summer. It's the perfect setup for me since I have weekends off with Kevin and during the school year, I have afternoons off with him too. I don't have to put him in daycare and that's a good thing. I took him away from home where his grandmothers would have been happy to share picking him up from school with each other so that they could take care of him while I finished work."

"I guess that is a really good thing about being a teacher." He glanced at her. "Maybe it's none of my business, but why did you take him away? I know you said you felt smothered."

She inhaled deeply and he glimpsed the strain on her face. "Because I think I mentioned I have a very strong-willed family. Well, it's my father. It took me a long time, and with Adam's help, for me to stand on my own feet and take control of my life. My father means well, but he has always been inclined to try to tell me what is best for me. To take over my life. And it was hard to get him to let go. I feared I was going to lose that independence that I'd fought so hard for. This job opening just reached out to me and I took it."

Levi shot her an assuring glance. "You aren't going to lose your independence. You have a determination about you that shows." He laughed as he watched the road. "Maybe once you struggled, but not anymore."

She laughed and he liked the sound of it. "I wish I was as certain as you sound."

"Believe me, I saw the look in your eyes back there in the coffee shop. You know what you need and you're standing firm. You're going to be okay, Jessica. And so is Kevin."

"Thanks for the vote of confidence."

"Anytime." He smiled and then turned onto a dirt road. It was in a remote area, overgrown, and the road was truly not much more than ruts but it was what Max wanted right now.

He looked away from the crowding greenery and saw her looking around skeptically. "Okay, I'll warn you about Max's place. It looks a little rough but it isn't as bad as it looks. He likes his privacy and his place is a work in progress."

"It looks very private." Jessica looked around at nothing but palm trees and vegetation.

"Hang on. It looks better around the next curve."

He followed the curve and the clearing opened up before them.

There was a gate; Levi jumped out and unlocked it and then jogged back to the Jeep. "It's private. And just as I said, a work in progress. But it suits Max."

They were driving through the trees as he spoke and Jessica found herself anticipating what she would see.

"Max is great with his hands. He likes building things. He's got a very small living space for now and is building his own home himself. It's a slow go because Max is in and out. We never know if he's going to be gone a week or three months."

She gasped as they drove around another curve onto a very small beach.

He smiled. "Pretty, huh?"

"Oh, I can see why he lives here. It's gorgeous."

Levi took in the beauty that he'd gotten used to but understood what she was thinking, seeing it for the first time. The water surrounding the island was a beautiful topaz but here it seemed a little deeper and the pale-blue sailboat tied to an anchor just offshore added to the picturesque view. A few colorful beach chairs sat haphazardly in the sand from the last time he and his brothers had all gathered for a campfire on the beach a couple of weeks ago.

"Is that his house?" She pointed toward the edge of the trees, where a shack of sorts nestled beneath the palms.

"That's it."

The land behind the small shack rose up slightly. A trail wandered among the natural groundcover to an area where a larger structure was being built. "And up there, partly hidden, is his work in progress."

"I love it," she said with a laugh in her voice. "And you're right—there's not much to the little house."

He parked and watched her study the shack. "It's made from salvaged wood and windows." It had a slanted roof and it, too, had been painted a faded blue. A standing paddleboard leaned against the wall, along with a surfboard, and to the side, a red kayak on a stand. A small table, chairs, and a barbecue pit were there also.

He enjoyed watching her and was glad he'd brought her out. He knew with every passing second, despite what she'd said about their incompatibility because of his job, that he wanted to get to know her. And spending time with her was the only way to do it.

Jessica was enjoying herself far too much as she got out of the truck and walked toward the perfect little shack. It looked like the perfect hideaway nestled into this tropical setting. Like a tiny shack one might see in a painting. Her imagination reeled with the romance of the place…okay, so she should haul her imagination away from some of those thoughts as her gaze drifted to Levi. He had walked ahead of her to the front door. *If the man had looked good in his uniform, he looked even better in T-shirt and shorts.*

She moved toward the side of the house to get a better look at the kayak and to put a little distance between her and Levi and hopefully her increasingly distracting thoughts about the man. A noise startled her. She stepped back and gasped when the underbrush rattled and shook. Suddenly, a wild pig burst through the underbrush. She screamed and stumbled back, and fell rump first into the sand.

The pig trotted straight to her and started to sniff her.

"Oh my goodness," she managed, happy she wasn't screaming from fright. And happy that it was soft sand she'd landed in.

"Are you all right?" Levi chuckled as he came to look down at her.

She stared up at him. "I'm fine. But is this pig safe?" It snorted as it pressed its black-whiskered nose against her ribs.

"Charlotte is safe. She's just checking you out. You didn't hurt yourself?"

"No, only my pride."

He held a hand out to her. "Don't let it be bruised on my behalf. Charlotte is some pig and getting away from her would be anyone's natural reaction."

She grasped his hand and felt the shiver of awareness travel through her as he pulled her to a standing position. Her heart pounded as she found herself brushing up against him as she stood.

"He didn't get very creative when he named her," Levi said, softly, as they stood there.

She felt breathless and pulled her gaze from his to study the pig in the same manner that the pig was studying her. "You're sure she's not going to bite me?"

"No, she's a good pig but they make great watchdogs. Pigs are very territorial and though she's not alerting anybody that you're here, she knows there's no one here to alert. But when Max is home, if he's up there working on the house or if he's inside the house and someone comes on the property, Charlotte lets him know."

Why did Max need such privacy and need to be alerted if someone was on his property? She was curious but not sure whether she should ask or not.

"Come on inside. I need to feed her and just check on things real quick and then we can leave."

He grabbed a key from under a rock near the side of the house. He unlocked the door and walked inside, and then stuck his head back out the door and looked at her. "It's okay. Come on in. You might find this interesting."

She followed him in. Charlotte trotted in beside her, nearly knocking her over in her haste to get inside the house. Jessica laughed watching the pig trot from the first room into another room at the back of the shack. The pig was snorting and grunting the whole time.

Levi grinned at her. "She's making sure everything is in its place and she's looking for Max."

"I can tell. Does he leave her often?"

"When he needs to, he has to. I try to get out here and check on her every few days, you know, for some food—but that's the thing about Charlotte. If I don't make it out every day, she can fend for herself. She eats fruits and there's plenty of food here for her to eat; she just has to forage for that. So it's not like he has a cat or dog and has to worry that if I get tied up or one of his other brothers gets tied up and nobody can make it out here, which has happened, that she's okay."

As he spoke, she studied the room. The furniture was handcrafted, it looked like. She walked over to the couch and studied the wood. It shone and was smooth to the touch, with brightly colored cushions forming the softer areas of the seating arrangement.

"This is beautiful."

"Max likes to do things with his hands. He's very talented."

She studied the bar that separated the small living room from what was a tiny, but well-equipped kitchen. It was as cozy as she'd imagined but cuter. The countertop was made of what looked like a huge piece of driftwood that had been sanded and lacquered for the flat surface. The underside was still the rough, interesting driftwood. The wall holding up the piece was painted a deep burgundy that was almost black and matched the tones in the kitchen area cabinets. The counters in the kitchen were made of stainless steel, it looked like, which made it a very functioning but low maintenance area. But the view of the beach from the old windows made it all perfect. "This is amazing."

"Yeah, it is. My brother is very talented and very much a minimalist when it comes to what he needs in his life. But it stands to reason since he's trained to live off the land and to survive on what's in his backpack."

"I get it."

"When he started building the home up the hill, I was surprised because it's pretty good-sized compared to this. But it still remains minimalistic when it comes to what most people in the States want in a home. Still, I think he's anticipating settling down one day. And so the house is probably more for that special someone he wants in his life. Though he's told me it's not any time soon."

"I am very impressed. Your brother sounds very interesting."

"Yes, he is." Levi lifted the lid of a metal trash can, pulled a bucket from it and filled it with feed. Charlotte hustled over to him, snorting and oinking excitedly. "But maybe I shouldn't have brought you out here to get impressed by my brother."

Levi hitched a dark brow at her and his lip hitched upward as he walked by.

She chuckled. "I'm impressed with you too," she added, despite the danger of letting herself act on the attraction she felt for him. She trailed him and Charlotte outside and watched as he poured the bucket of food into a carved-out wooden trough on the other side of the barbecue pit. Immediately, Charlotte began to eat.

He set the bucket down and stared at her. Instantly, the attraction that simmered very near the surface between them reignited and she was breathless. He took two steps to her and looked into her eyes. Her chest suddenly ached and a lump formed in her throat. He was taller than her but not too tall; if she walked into his arms right now, her head would fit nicely against his shoulder. She shook the thought away; she swallowed the sudden longing and refused to let herself look away as he lifted his hand and touched his thumb to her cheek.

Sudden tears ached in her chest at his gentle touch.

And as his thumb brushed slowly along her cheek line, she couldn't move.

"You had some sand on your cheek."

Butterflies cascaded through her and all she could

do was nod. He swallowed hard; his Adam's apple bobbed—*Adam.* Her husband's face flashed across her memory as Levi let his hand drop and he quickly reentered the house. She just stood there, unable to move, as her world seemed to collide in so many directions.

She heard him lift the metal trash can lid and heard the bucket hit the feed as he dropped it inside, followed by the metal on metal as he replaced the lid. Her heart hammered as confusion and longing rolled through her.

She was still unstable when he came back outside and locked the door. She watched him replace the key under the rock and then turned to look at her. He seemed perfectly fine.

But she knew that she wasn't. Something about Levi Sinclair got to her.

He stood a good five feet from her and he had rammed his fingertips into the pockets of his shorts and looked restrained.

"I guess we'll head back." But he made no move

to leave or to come closer to her.

They stared at each other. So many thoughts ran through her mind, thoughts she hadn't had in so long. She realized she should feel guilty but at the moment guilt wasn't what she was feeling.

CHAPTER NINE

What was he doing? Levi had asked himself that question from the moment he had entered the coffee shop and saw her there. Had asked himself that question again every mile he had driven out toward Max's place. And now he knew he was in trouble. They hadn't had that many conversations. They hadn't spent that much time together. And yet there was no denying that something he had never felt before gripped him when he was near Jessica, not only just when he thought of her. And when he looked at her, it was undeniable what feelings swamped him. He wanted her. Physically, oh yeah, but more…he wanted her in his life. He'd never, ever felt anything like the emotion that had roared through him and now clasped him in its tight grasp.

He needed to hold her. To touch her. He needed to take the burdens she felt and place them on his own shoulders. He needed her…needed to be the man she needed.

He sank chest-deep in trouble.

He cleared his throat. "I guess we better get back. Kevin will be waiting."

"Yes," she said and he heard the crack in her words. They came gruff, slightly hoarse.

His chest tightened and nothing on earth could stop him as he took a step toward her. Then, he stopped and forced himself to turn toward the truck.

She was off-limits.

She had sorrow to overcome and a life to get in order and had made it perfectly clear that she was not looking for romantic entanglements.

His problem was he was already entangled.

CHAPTER TEN

They talked about Roscoe and Jaco all the way back to the coffee shop where her car was parked. She noticed and was just as careful as he was to make sure that they talked only about the dogs. Even Kevin wasn't a safe conversation for them considering he was the instigator of this whole troubled web.

If she let herself, there was so much that she could want from Levi.

But it had only been two years since Adam's death and until she met Levi, she'd believed that hadn't been long enough for her to want a relationship. *This was too soon. How could she even feel anything remotely near what she was feeling?*

Levi parked the truck behind her car. She fumbled to unbuckle her seat belt as the truck was still rolling. The moment it came to a stop, she opened her door. "Thanks," she said. "It was fun."

Her feet touched the pavement as she spoke but his hand wrapped around her arm, stopping her.

"Wait."

She looked back at him, felt his touch burning into her skin. "Okay," she managed.

"My mom's birthday is Saturday and the whole family is getting together. Would you and Kevin like to come with me? Everyone would like to meet you."

Her skin where his hand touched was on fire and her stomach had slipped to her toes. She felt unsteady as she started to shake her head.

"Come," he urged her, his voice gruff as his gaze bore into hers.

Despite everything telling her to run, she could not look away. She could not run.

And instead, she nodded. "What time?" *What was*

she doing?

Friday after school, Lana and Jessica were cleaning up in the classroom while Kevin played on the playground with one of the other teacher's sons. Jessica straightened up the papers on her desk and glanced out the window every few moments to make sure that Kevin was where he was supposed to be playing on the swings and the slide.

Jessica had told Lana about her trip out to Max's place with Levi. And to her surprise, although Lana told her she was glad that she was stepping out, she also cautioned her to be careful.

"So are you ready for tomorrow?" Lana stood, arms crossed, and with a serious expression as she studied Jessica.

"No. I am a nervous wreck. Why did I agree to this? I didn't need this in my life, Lana. I was just getting my life straight. And now..." She shook her head, thinking. "What am I doing?"

"You've been nervous all week. That's why I

haven't been saying much. I've been trying to stay out of your life. I've been trying to let you think this out. And have some space. But I can't stand it. I feel like I'm the one who pushed you to do this and now I'm worried I pushed too soon." Lana gave a shaky laugh. "My daddy has a saying—I'm sending you out to a rodeo and you ain't ready to ride the bull yet."

Jessica laughed despite the turmoil inside her. "Your daddy must be a hoot."

Lana rolled her eyes. "My daddy and all my brothers—or stinkers is what they are. Hard-riding cattlemen who are stubborn and irritating as a burr in my saddle. But I still love them and honestly, I miss them. Sometimes they had words of wisdom that are so true, like this statement. I can't tell you how many times my daddy said that to me over the years. You know, my mama died early and my daddy raised me as best he could, but being a man and with the houseful of guys, he never felt like he knew what to do with me. He always felt like he was sending me out to the world unprepared. And I kind of feel like that's what I'm doing to you right now. I want you to find love again,

Jessica, but I sure hope I'm not pushing you to do something too soon."

Jessica watched Kevin climb to the top of the ladder on the playground and then he slid down with a huge grin plastered across his face. She could tell he was happy.

Happy was an understatement. He had been overjoyed when she had told him they were going to go with Levi to a party tomorrow.

"I keep telling myself that these feelings that I feel toward Levi are just normal. It's because I haven't let myself even think about anything that has to do with romance or falling in love again since Adam died. But there's the whole issue of why Levi? And he's a police officer. It's too dangerous."

Lana grimaced. "Your hearts spoke to each other. And I didn't really realize how strongly you felt the pull when I first pushed you to have an open heart and not run away from feeling again. Now I feel a little bit responsible, like my daddy must have felt raising me."

Despite her worrying, Jessica chuckled, glad to have something humorous to think about for the moment. "I can only imagine how it must have felt being raised by a rodeo daddy and with five older brothers."

Lana rolled her eyes and drawled in her best Texas cowgirl twang, "Honey, they smothered me with love, I can tell you that."

"But you made it. I will too. Stop worrying. Ryan and Jillian will be there, and I'll get to meet Jillian's family. I'm just going to enjoy the afternoon and let Kevin and Roscoe play with Jaco." All she had to do was keep telling herself that.

"How's it going with Jessica?" Ryan asked Levi on Friday afternoon. It had been a busy few days at work. "You've been pacing this office like a caged lion. Jillian and Jessica had coffee yesterday. She said she's coming to your mom's birthday party with you and you haven't said a word. Jillian really likes Jessica."

Levi cupped his hands on the desk in front of him and shot a narrow gaze at his brother-in-law. "I'm not sure where it's going. It's complicated." That was the understatement of the year.

"So how are you and Jillian doing on the baby quest?" He felt for his sister, knowing she might not be able to have a child if it didn't happen in the near future.

"Actually, she's been seeing the doctor lately and we're waiting to hear results from the test today." Ryan smiled. "I'm hoping I have good news when I go home. Man, I'm tense myself."

Levi grinned. "So do you have any idea, any good feeling about what the doctor might say?"

Ryan shrugged. "No but I really hope for Jillian's sake that the doc gives her good news. Then she'll have the perfect present for your mom tomorrow. But, we're going to adopt if we don't get pregnant the biological way. Jillian really wants to carry at least one baby herself and experience what that feels like. Even if it's just one and then we adopt all of our other children."

"I hope she gets to do that." Levi's thoughts went to himself on that one. He hadn't thought about being a daddy. He had been busy thinking about his career and thinking that eventually he would get to the family portion of his life. But to really think about fathering a child and holding that little baby in his arms and knowing that it was a part of him? He hadn't thought about that. But now when he contemplated fatherhood, he thought about Kevin and Jessica.

"What are you thinking about?" Ryan asked.

Levi realized he had been so deep in thought, he'd zoned out. "Just thinking about life. It's not always fair. You and Jillian understand that—you're old enough—but Kevin, poor little boy's just a kid."

"Yeah, you're right. So I think his mother is wise to move slow. I just hope she gives you a fair shot." Ryan stood and walked over to the coffee pot.

"Me too." Levi was really going to have to think about the best way to proceed because if there was ever a time to be wise his entire life, this was it.

Ryan's phone rang. He spun to look at Levi and then he whipped his phone from his pocket. "It's Jillian. I'll take this outside. Be right back."

Levi went and poured himself a cup of coffee. He watched Ryan pace out on the sidewalk and prayed for the best.

"He's here, Momma! And Jaco's with him!" Kevin exclaimed the next morning. He'd been waiting at the window for an hour despite her telling him it was early.

Before she could stop him, Kevin yanked the door open and raced outside.

"Kevin!" she called. She grabbed her purse from the hall table and a plate of fudge she'd made and then followed him outside. She reached the front steps just in time to see her son throw himself into Levi's arms and give him a huge hug.

The scene had her stopping in her tracks and her heart cracked into a thousand pieces.

Caution.

Caution was the word and action of the day. Her son's heart was at stake. That was much more important than her own heart.

Levi stood and smiled. His eyes bore into hers. He looked so good. She had missed him. But that wasn't important right now. Kevin was and she better remember that.

"Hey there," he said, his voice low, gentle.

Her heart thundered against her ribs. "Hi. Are you sure you're ready for this? Kevin and Roscoe are about to explode with excitement."

Kevin grinned. "It is going to be a *grrreeat* day! I can hardly stand it, I'm so excited."

That was the understatement of the year and despite all the turmoil inside her, Jessica laughed.

Levi's eyes twinkled as they met hers and he gently tousled Kevin's short hair.

"Everybody's excited to meet you, too, little buddy. Let's load up." He picked Kevin up and placed him into the backseat of the truck.

She pulled the booster seat from the backseat of her car and started toward his truck. He hurried toward her.

"I'll take that," he said, striding to her. He took it; their hands brushed and her stomach trembled as she quickly let go. "Have you had a good week?" he asked, as if he'd felt nothing.

"I've had a great week," she quipped, not

admitting that she'd been tied in knots all week. "How about you?"

"Oh, great," he said over his shoulder as he put the seat in the truck and reached around to fasten it.

She watched the play of muscles across his back and decided she'd be better off to get into the truck instead of watching him. She hopped into the front seat, yanked the seat belt across her and snapped it tight. *The man had had a great week—he'd probably slept like a baby in his sexy body, while she'd hardly slept at all.* She was feeling quite grumpy as he drove and knew this was not how she needed to be feeling.

Levi chattered as they traveled past the Windswept Bay Resort and turned onto Oceanview Drive as it followed along the coast. The sparkling blue water called to her as they rode with the windows open. The dogs both had their heads hanging out each side of the truck. The salty air helped ease the butterflies that were in an uproar throughout her.

"My family is looking forward to meeting both of you," Levi said.

"I'm looking forward to meeting them too," Kevin called from the backseat. Jessica looked back at her son. He had one hand on Roscoe's back and one hand on Jaco's back, and he was grinning from ear to ear.

Jessica would have laughed if she weren't so scared she was taking her son in the deep water of heartache if she wasn't careful. She had to get a grip.

Levi reached across the console and placed his hand on her forearm, drawing her to look at him. "Relax," he said. "Just relax. You've been tense since I arrived."

How did he know that? Did he also know she was about to have a heartburn attack?

"Yeah, Momma—relax." Kevin mimicked his new hero. "All she does is worry, worry, worry." Kevin held his hands up in exaggeration of a six-year-old.

Jessica groaned. Any other time, she'd have laughed. Now she was too busy trying to ignore the warmth of Levi's hand on her forearm.

Levi chuckled too and smiled at her as he gently squeezed her arm before he placed his hand back on the steering wheel. The warmth of his touch lingered, as did the tingle of awareness.

"I think she worries because she wants everything to be perfect for everybody around her. My mom was that way and she had nine kids."

Kevin's mouth fell open. "*Nine kids?* You have that many brothers and sisters?"

Levi laughed. "Yes, there's a bunch of us."

"Wow. That's why you will be a good daddy because you'll know how to get me some brothers and sisters. My friend Percy told me that getting a daddy was the way I could get a little brother like he just got."

Jessica gasped and she closed her eyes in disbelief. Levi's hand touched her arm again.

"So now I understand." He gave her arm a gentle caress. "It's all going to be okay." He patted her arm and she looked at him in total bewilderment. "Stop worrying," he murmured and then louder so Kevin could hear, "Come on, let's go meet everyone. You're going to like my brothers."

"I know I will. Because I like you."

Levi reached over the truck seat and patted Kevin's knee. "And I like you because you're a good kid. Unbuckle and let's go have some fun."

Jessica got out of the truck but the only place she wanted to go now was home.

CHAPTER ELEVEN

Moments later, she was being introduced to Violet and Sam Sinclair, Levi's parents.

Sam reminded her of Levi. "Welcome. We're glad you're here."

"Yes, I'm so thrilled to meet you." Violet gave her a hug. "And you must be Kevin?"

"That's me." Kevin grinned. "I'm Kevin, and I like your house on the ocean. We have to walk to the ocean from my house."

Violet chuckled. "You remind me of my boys. I bet you keep your mom guessing." She looked at

Jessica.

Kevin looked from her to Violet and then to Levi. "Can I go outside with the dogs?"

Levi looked at her. "Do you mind?"

"No, not at all." She wasn't sure after what Kevin had said earlier whether it was a good idea or not, but how could she refuse now?

"Jessica," Jillian called and rushed toward her.

Levi waved fingers at Jessica and then led Kevin to the patio doors. They went out onto the porch, where there was a small gathering of men.

Jillian hugged her. "I am so excited you're here. And with Levi. I know you're just here but I've got to tell you, Levi doesn't bring women around. My brother is so busy being police chief that he puts himself on the back burner. Yes, I know, I know—this is not a date. He has already informed me as such. But I'm still glad to see you two spending time together."

Jessica wanted to ask her about her doctor appointment but decided not to ask until they were alone. Moments later, Jillian's sisters surrounded her. Shar and Olivia were Jillian's triplets and though

Jillian and Olivia were blonde and almost identical, Shar was brunette and had a look all her own. Cali was a couple of years older and beautiful.

She winked. "This is so exciting. Levi hasn't brought a date to a family gathering in forever."

"Oh, this isn't a date," Jessica told her.

"Looks like a date to me," Shar said. "And Levi looked like he might be confused about it too."

"No pressure." Olivia shook her head at her sisters. "We're all hoping for him to settle down. He doesn't know he's ready but he is."

"But really—it isn't." Jessica tried again.

Shar pushed her dark hair behind her ear and rolled her eyes. "I'll just say what we're all thinking. It's about time he started thinking about himself. That man works his tail off for our community and he looks genuinely relaxed today. And I think that's because of you."

Violet moved to stand beside Jessica. "Okay, girls, back off. We don't want to scare Jessica off. Let's take her over here and give her something to sip on." Linking her arm in Jessica's, Violet walked her over to the kitchen area, where a feast was laid out.

"I almost forgot to wish you happy birthday," Jessica said, having forgotten her manners completely with all the different things being thrown her way just now.

Violet shot her a sideways glance and looked very happy. "Thank you. Celebrating my birthday is a good excuse to have my family come home every year. Although my Max is who knows where right now, and Cam must have gotten tied up on his trip. I haven't heard from him yet. Texas is a long way away when it comes to family gatherings. But he's happy there, so this mama can deal with that."

"I know how you feel. Kevin being happy is the most important thing to me. I can handle him growing up and moving away from me if that's where his life takes him and he's happy."

The thought had Jessica thoughtful for a moment.

One day Kevin would be an adult and very well could move somewhere away from her. The idea was hard on her. Her gaze went to the window, where she could see him playing down by the beach with Roscoe and Levi.

"I've been lucky that Cam is the only child not living near me. Cali and Olivia lived away but both came home to roost."

"Cam probably won't be doing that, Mom," Jillian warned.

"Not Cam," Shar agreed. "He might have been born in Florida but like the saying goes, 'he got to Texas as fast as he could.'"

"That's the truth," Jillian told her.

Jessica smiled. "My friend Lana is from Texas. She's my co-teacher at school. Her family owns a big ranch there in Texas and I get tickled when she talks about her dad and her five cowboy brothers. They weren't happy about her coming to Florida."

Olivia got a twinkle in her eyes. "Maybe we need to introduce her to Cam next time he's in town."

"That might be fun," Jessica said. "I'm not sure she's looking for a way back home, though."

Violet chuckled. "Maybe it could be Cameron's way back home."

"No, Mom, you know Cam's not ever leaving his

ranch. He'll come visit but that cowboy loves his ranch."

"On the other hand," Shar said. "It would take a herd of wild horses to drag Levi from Windswept Bay. That man will marry and grow old here on the bay." Everybody's gazes locked onto Jessica and suddenly she felt very exposed.

"You know," she stammered. "I'm not really looking for a relationship either. At least not right now. But I think Levi is a wonderful man. I'm just not ready."

"I've already told them that," Jillian said. "But there's always hope. And you never know when love will strike. And I can tell you that when it does, it has a way of changing timetables while exchanging minds and hearts."

Jillian's sisters all nodded agreement.

"I don't want him or any of you to get false hopes." Jessica was starting to worry as she felt the pressure of matchmaking surrounding her.

Violet smiled. "Ignore us. We are showing very bad manners. You're very smart to move with caution.

I think you're a good mom to worry about such things and I love the way that you're not jumping into something. Your heart has to heal."

"Did I miss the party?" a deep voice called and Violet gasped and spun toward the foyer.

"Cam," Violet exclaimed as a handsome man with a cowboy hat walked into the room.

"Hey, Mom. I didn't miss the party, did I?"

Violet moved across the room and into his arms. Delight lit her expression.

Jessica's heart clutched and tears welled in her eyes watching the sweet exchange. She looked immediately back out the window to watch Levi and Kevin running along the beach down below the house with the dogs. Two other men were with them who she'd seen at the Thanksgiving celebration and knew were Levi's brothers. One looked like Levi. She'd heard he had a twin but hadn't thought much about it until seeing them together.

"That's Jake and Trent. Trent is Levi's twin," Violet said. "It looks like they're having fun with Kevin."

"Yes, it does." She was happy for Violet. All her kids were home to celebrate with her but Max.

Moments later, all the guys came inside, with Kevin chattering excitedly with Jake and Trent. Levi sought her out immediately and she felt a warm glow fill her, as if she'd just stepped into the morning sunshine after a stormy winter's night…

She looked away and caught Jillian watching her. The twinkle in her friend's eyes told Jessica that Jillian did not believe she and Levi were just friends.

"How are you doing?" Levi asked as he went to stand beside Jessica. She probably didn't even realize that her eyes were huge as he entered the room. *What had she been lost in thought about when he and Kevin walked in?*

"I'm doing great. And Cam's here, which has made your mom so happy."

"Yes, that would do it. If Max had been here, everything would be perfect."

As everyone filled the room, coming inside from

all directions, Levi moved closer to Jessica, standing slightly behind her as his brothers-in-law moved to stand beside his sisters. Jillian and Ryan moved to stand beside the birthday cake.

The soft scent of Jessica's hair drew him closer as he leaned in and whispered in her ear, "She's about to get happier."

"Is this what I think it is?" Jessica turned her face to his quickly, bringing their lips almost crashing into each other.

It happened so quickly he didn't have time to move away, and had to force himself not to lean into her, closing the space between them and feeling her lips pressed to his. He swallowed hard and wondered whether his eyes had grown as wide as hers as she realized they were almost kissing.

"Mom," Jillian said, excitement in her tone. "You are going to be a grandmother." Jillian's voice broke with emotion as she said the words.

Levi had learned earlier in the day, through Ryan, that his sister had found out she was having a baby and he was thrilled for them. As was the entire family.

Everyone moved to give Jillian a hug and to congratulate them.

"I am so happy for you," Jessica said, giving Jillian a hug and then Ryan. Kevin had been sitting with Jake since they'd come in from outside but launched himself at Ryan.

"When will your baby get here?"

Ryan gave her son a hug and Jessica marveled at how Kevin had attached himself to the men of this family. And they were all being so gentle and kind to him. Ryan hugged him and crouched down.

"Well, Kevin, it'll be about eight months from now. Are you going to come spend some time with him when he arrives?"

"I sure am. I can babysit him."

Ryan chuckled. "Well, you won't exactly be old enough for that but he will definitely like you coming over to play with him."

Kevin's expression lit up like a Christmas tree. "I can take him to show-and-tell."

That got laughter from everyone.

Later after the cake and punch had been eaten,

Levi drove Jessica and a very sleepy Kevin back home.

Even the dogs had curled up in the seat on either side of Kevin.

"It was a wonderful night," Jessica said softly.

"I'm glad you and Kevin came." In the darkness of the cab, Levi felt contentment surround him. "I really mean that, Jessica."

He heard her almost silent sigh beside him. "I'm glad we came too."

CHAPTER TWELVE

By the time they got home, Kevin could barely hold his eyes open. Jessica led the way into the house while Levi carried her son behind her. She unlocked the door and led him through the house to Kevin's bedroom and watched as Levi gently laid her little boy in his bed. She fought not to let her emotions get involved but seeing the way Levi was so careful with him touched her heart once again.

She removed Kevin's shoes and quickly changed him into his pajamas. She was tugging his pajama top over his head with Levi's help holding him up when

Kevin opened his eyes and smiled at Levi.

"This was fun tonight." Then he leaned back on his bed and snuggled into the covers.

She met Levi's gaze and he smiled. His eyes were serious as he looked down at her son and then back at her. "You have a great kid here, Jess."

Her heart clutched, as it had been doing so often around Levi. *Adam had called her Jess.*

She led the way back into the living room, not exactly sure of the emotions fluttering through her like the wings of a thousand butterflies. "Can I make some coffee?"

He stood close to her in the hall and she was so very aware of him.

"I would love that, if you're sure."

"I would really like that." And she meant it. So many emotions and feelings crowded inside her chest at the moment and she just didn't want to be alone right now. Maybe it was because she had just spent so much time with his large family. Maybe spending time with his family made her miss her family. Made her miss all the times she and Adam had spent with their families.

All of the above, but really, she just wanted to spend some time with Levi. Just for a few moments.

"I'll go get the dogs and let them play in the backyard while you make the coffee."

"That would be great."

A few minutes later, he came back inside and she had taken two cups out of the cabinet. The scent of coffee filled the air. Levi came back into the kitchen and leaned against the counter. The kitchen seemed suddenly smaller with his presence.

She filled the cups with coffee and remembered that he liked his black, like she liked hers. "Here you go." She handed him a cup. Their fingers brushed as he took it from her and that tingle of awareness danced up her arm. She moved quickly away and picked up her own cup, holding it between her hands. She leaned against the counter and met his eyes once more over the brim. The rich scent of the coffee surrounded her, she wished like a shield—a shield of protection against the emotions tightening inside her. She watched his fingertips move in gentle circles on the cup before he took a sip and her thoughts went to his gentle touch on her arm earlier as they had driven to his parents' home. She shivered involuntarily.

He set his cup down on the counter and moved to her. "Are you cold?"

He was so close, she gripped her cup tightly, holding it between them. "No, I'm not." Her pulse pounded and her mouth went dry as he took her cup and set it on the counter beside her. And then he leaned in and brushed his lips over hers.

Every fiber of her soul trembled at the touch of his lips. Her knees weakened like putty and she moved closer. His arms went around her and drew her against his chest.

"I don't want to scare you, Jessica, but you should know that I have feelings for you. This is no casual date."

She didn't even bother to say this wasn't supposed to be a date; instead, she snuggled into him and lifted her face to his. "Could you kiss me again?" She slid her arms around him. She didn't have to ask twice. Levi's arms held her tight as he lowered his lips again to hers and this time the kiss took her breath away.

She could feel his heartbeat thundering against her own, feel his muscles in his back tense at her touch and knew that he was fighting to hold in his emotions, just as she was.

His lips were firm and warm and ignited a firestorm in her. She was breathless when he lifted his head and looked into her eyes.

"I think I better go for tonight."

She didn't want him to. "Can you just hold me for a little longer?" It had been so long since she'd known the feel of loving arms around her. And she wasn't sure she could give them up again.

"Honey, I can hold you as long as you want me to."

Jessica breathed in his scent and laid her head against his shoulder. She could stay like that forever, she realized.

"I care for you, Levi." The words were muffled against his shirt but still clear, and she felt him stiffen and grow still.

He kissed her forehead. "We'll go as slow as you

need us to go. But that makes me happy."

"I can't promise you anything," she said. "I'm scared out of my wits but I can't deny that I have feelings for you."

He smiled. "Music to my ears." And then he took her hand and led her to the living room. He sat on the couch and pulled her down into his arms and then he kissed her again.

Jessica's heart felt so full of joy as she gave in to the kiss and the emotions she felt for Levi. They would go slow, but having admitted that she felt something more than just attraction for this wonderful man was a step in the right direction.

Wasn't it?

She just had to ignore all the negative voices in her head. The ones saying he was a police officer, his job was too dangerous and the voice that repeated again and again that her heart wasn't ready.

The day after her mother's birthday party, Jillian walked into the office she shared with her sisters Cali and Olivia at Windswept Bay Resort. She had what she considered an extraordinary promotion idea for the resort and was excited to share it with her sisters. Of course, these days, since finding out she was carrying a baby in her womb, everything was exciting and joyous to her. She was practically floating with happiness and wanted everyone she knew to feel such amazing joy. And maybe that was why this idea had slipped into her dreams last night.

The resort had been focusing on weddings and had been doing great, but her idea might jumpstart more weddings for the upcoming year. She had called and asked all of her sisters to be at the meeting. She had asked Shar to attend too even though she no longer worked in the resort office. She worked full-time with her sea turtle rescue foundation that she and Gage had founded after their wedding. But she wanted Shar to be at the meeting to get her input because it involved their brothers.

Especially Levi.

It was nine o'clock when she walked in and everyone was arriving at the same time. "Hey, everyone. I'm so excited about this and glad you are all here."

Cali pulled her jacket off and put it behind her seat. "You sound so excited I can't wait to hear what's on your mind."

"I feel the same way." Olivia walked in, dropped her purse in her chair and went straight to the coffee pot. "And you're being so secretive. Shoot."

Jillian hadn't told any of them anything over the phone—despite every one of them pushing for more information.

Shar was still in her jogging suit, and had probably just come in from jogging along the beach, where she was always on the lookout for sea turtle nests first thing in the mornings. "I'm all ears and really, really curious. So spill the beans, sista."

Jillian laughed, she was so excited. "Okay, because I can't stand it any longer I'm just going to shoot straight. I want to have a Valentine Bachelor Auction here at the resort as a PR campaign for the resort. And the biggie is I want to have our brothers involved as some of the bachelors. But, most especially, Levi."

Her sisters' expressions were instantly enthusiastic and everyone began to talk at once.

"This is such an awesome idea." Cali's smile was brilliant.

"Amazing!" Olivia nearly dropped the coffee pot.

"Oh yeah," Shar growled and pumped her fist in the air while she laughed and nodded her head. "Levi will *kill* us and yet it is totally perfect and worth it."

"I agree on all levels." Jillian tried to control her excitement. "Maybe it's because I'm so happy, with marrying Ryan and now finding out that I'm going to have the baby—both of my dreams come true—I just can't not do this. At Mom's birthday, I felt that there was something between Levi and Jessica. When Ryan and I suggested to Kevin that Levi would be perfect as his class show-and-tell, we both had in our mind that Jessica and Levi might be a good idea. And then at the party, they were there together, and you tell me if you didn't see something between them?"

"I thought there was something," Shar said. "Levi looked at Jessica across the room and you could feel his heart beating."

"BJ and I talked about it on the way home," Olivia said. "Even though we both had been hoping that when his sister comes for a visit soon that maybe she and Levi would be a match, we ditched that idea because he looked pretty snared by Jessica." She laughed. "Of course, we do have five brothers, so maybe if she ever has a break in her work with the wildlife parks and gets here for a visit, maybe one of them will still be available."

Shar shot a question look at Olivia. "Are you two getting into the matchmaking business?"

"Maybe," Jillian said. "I'm sure one of our brothers will be available and if it's meant to be for one of them to fall for BJ's sister, then it will happen."

"Right," Olivia agreed.

"Shar," Jillian added, "I'm not really thinking matchmaking for the guys but I can't help thinking that because of what Jessica has been through, she might need a little incentive."

Cali frowned. "You might be right about that, since she lost her husband and moving forward might be hard for her. But are you sure auctioning off Levi will help that? He might get bought by someone completely different, *if* we're able to talk him into it in the first place."

"I thought of that. I'm thinking that it can go a few different ways. If she doesn't bid on him and someone else gets him, then maybe that will push her to move forward and even fight for him if she feels threatened—"

Shar broke in excitedly, "And of course she would only feel threatened if she is interested but having trouble moving forward."

"Right. Does that make sense?"

Her sisters all grinned at her.

Olivia's eyes narrowed. "What has happened to our quiet Jillian? I never knew you had such a devious mind." She laughed.

"Like real devious," Shar agreed with emphasis, obviously enjoying the aspect of Jillian coming out of the shadows of her sisters.

"But she has sweet intentions." Cali smiled thoughtfully. "I see exactly what you're thinking and I think it's a wonderful idea. I went through a hideous divorce and had trouble moving forward, so in a completely different manner I know moving toward a new future isn't always as easy as it seems."

"But you cared for Grant." Jillian smiled.

"I did and that changed everything…though it wasn't easy. I'm one hundred percent on board. As the PR person for the resort, I thank you for coming up with an amazing PR promotion that I didn't have to come up with. This is going to be so fun. After the huge Christmas season and boatload of weddings we had here, this might supercharge the summer wedding season."

Olivia paused, her coffee nearly to her lips. "Goodness—think about it. This is only the end of January. That gives all the auctioned-off bachelors and their buyers time to fall in love and book a wedding at the resort they met at." She laughed. "I am totally in. Let's do this."

"I'm going to add in my buddies down at the Sea Turtle Hospital into the bachelor pit." She laughed, sounding a little devious herself. "John and Alex are both bachelors. And obviously are devoting time rescuing sea turtles and not spending time cultivating dating opportunities." She beamed mischievously. "I feel the need to help out—with at least getting them a date and maybe something will happen."

Everyone laughed and looked genuinely thrilled. "This is going to be fun," Jillian said, so happy her sisters were on board with the project. "So, when should we start planning?"

Cali looked around the room. "I say let's do this and dig in now. We have less than two weeks and that's not a huge time frame to get this off and running and advertised."

Instantly everyone agreed and to Jillian's great delight, the planning began right then and there. Their brothers were going to either blow gaskets or play along for the fun of it. She figured the ones or one who blew the gasket was whose heart was starting to long to settle down.

Either way, it was going to be a great Valentine promotion.

CHAPTER THIRTEEN

"Wait, *what?*" Levi glared at his sister, certain he'd just heard wrong about what his sisters were concocting.

Smiling jubilantly—as if she knew something he didn't know—Jillian looked from him to her husband. "It's going to be a fantastic, fun time and will benefit the resort with all the publicity Cali is lining up with this Valentine Bachelor Auction. Tell him, Ryan."

Ryan looked both amused and skeptical. "Honey, I know you're excited. But you've put your brother in the hot seat and he has a different view from where he's sitting."

"Ya think?" Levi snapped.

Ryan was enjoying this. "He did just have a classroom of first graders tell him their moms were going to be upset if he was getting married. Riots could break out over Levi." Ryan laughed so hard his shoulders shook.

Levi crossed his arms over his chest. "I'm really glad you find this funny."

"I'm trying not to—honest, I am. But the more I think about it, the funnier it gets. Jillian, I can see the headlines now: 'Catfight at the Windswept Bay Resort Over the Sinclair Brothers'! Who knows? It might make national news."

Levi watched his sister's eyes widen. "National news could be great."

What was Ryan thinking, egging this on? But he had to admit that if the shoe was on the other foot, he would find it pretty entertaining—men enjoyed watching their friends in the hot seat.

The problem was he was just now making progress with Jessica. There was no way she would be bidding on him at the auction. *Would she?*

"Ignore Ryan. This is for a good cause and it's just dinner. You'll be helping us out and who knows, you could even get a date you enjoy going out with. If not, it's just dinner."

Levi rubbed the bridge of his nose. His sisters worked really hard to get the family resort running and profitable, and if he could help out, he could sacrifice one evening for that.

"Fine." He groaned. "You know I can't refuse to help out. But I don't have to like it."

Jillian put her arms around his neck and kissed him on the cheek. "I love you, big brother. I knew you would." She stepped back and looked at him. "How's it going with Jessica?"

"You ask that after you set me up?"

"Well, yes. Do you think she might bid on you?"

"We're friends."

"I thought I saw something a little more interesting than friends pass between the two of you at Mom's."

He cocked his head to the side and studied her.

"And so you decided to do a Valentine Bachelor Auction and throw me into the fray? That's real helpful of you."

A twinkle lit her eyes. "Maybe a little competition or pressure is a good thing. Jessica might decide to bid on someone and maybe she would bid on you."

"We've only known each other for a couple of weeks. Give me some time here. Besides, I don't see Jessica as the bidding type at a bachelor auction. And that may be one of the things I like about her." The woman in the grocery store came to mind.

Jessica backed away toward the door, smiling. "I guess we won't know until February 14." She chuckled and waved, blew Ryan a kiss and then walked out the door.

Betty Lou poked her head around the door of the dispatcher's room. "I think I'm going to have to come to that Valentine auction myself to see who bids on you. I might bid on you myself and help the fireworks."

Levi's brow dipped into a frown in automatic response to his sixty-something-year-old dispatcher.

"Betty Lou, if it gets bad, I might pay you to jump into the fray and buy me out of it."

She grinned. "Hey, that's an idea. I can be bought for a price. Otherwise I might just have to sit back and watch you suffer." She winked and then went back to her dispatching.

Ryan's shoulders shook; he was laughing so hard while trying not to make a sound as he watched Levi through splayed fingers across his face. He pulled his hand away. "The entertainment factor on this is going to be worth selling tickets to. I might have to start a raffle."

"I think I'm about to say something I never thought I would say. But right now I wish the paparazzi would come back to town and give me something to do other than to sit here and listen to you tease me about this auction."

"Well, hold onto that thought because if catfights break out over you, the paparazzi might show back up and put you on the front of the tabloids."

"Hey, now. That's too scary to even contemplate.

Oh gee, look—my shift is over." Levi stood, grabbed his keys off the desk and then headed for the door. "You and Baker have a good evening holding the fort down. I'll see you in the morning."

He heard Ryan's chuckles as the door closed behind him. This had been a crazy day—even before Jillian had come into the office. He'd had a drunk driver hit a tree—better that than an innocent family— then had a disturbance at the marina when a tourist decided a charter captain had cheated him—which hadn't happened. And then a petty theft at the grocery store. A bunch of odd little events…making Jillian's scheme fit right in.

He'd been thinking a lot about Jessica. It had been two days since he saw her. Two days since he kissed her and she had admitted that she could have feelings for him.

Two days too long.

He was ready to see her, despite the fact that he had made himself stay away to try to give her time to adjust to the feelings she had admitted to. But staying away had been hard and he wasn't sure he could stay away any longer. He missed her, and Kevin too.

He dialed her number as he got into the SUV.

"Hello, Levi," she answered on the first ring, her voice soft.

Warmth curled through him. "I've missed you," he said, not even bothering with hello.

"Oh," she almost whispered. "I-I've missed you too."

"Would you, Kevin, and Roscoe want to have a picnic dinner at the beach this evening? Me and Jaco could use some company."

He tensed, wondering whether she'd say yes. There was a pause.

"We would like that."

Yes, he wanted to shout. He felt more like a kid than the police chief of Windswept Bay. "Great. How about I pick you all up in about an hour?" It was five now so that would be six and give them a few hours before dark.

"That sounds perfect."

"Perfect," he said. And it was.

"This is a great idea," Kevin hollered at the top of his lungs as he jumped from the truck into the sand. Both dogs followed him. They raced toward the water; Kevin laughed when Roscoe gently tackled him in the sand and Jaco, with his big puppy paws, rolled in the sand with them.

Jessica's heart squeezed as she watched Kevin jump up and tear along the water's edge, chasing seagulls along with the dogs. She had been in turmoil since admitting to Levi that she felt something for him. Since kissing him and cuddling with him the night of the birthday party.

She had admitted to Lana what had happened and her friend had been overjoyed.

Jessica was in such an odd place. Joy, excitement, trepidation, and worry all intertwined together into a mixture that billowed around inside her with the wind force of a hurricane. And yet the moment Levi had called and asked them to come for a picnic on the beach, she had instantly said yes.

Now, a sense of anticipation filled her as his gaze rested on her. *Oh, what a confusing web wove around her heart.*

Levi grabbed the picnic basket from the bed of the truck, looking better than he needed to look if he were to help her get over the anticipation of kissing him again. He was not helping her…because she wanted him to. It was true.

"I'm glad you came. I've missed you and Kevin." He smiled and handed her a Frisbee and a kite. "I thought Kevin might enjoy us playing with these with him."

A lump lodged hard in her chest as Jessica took the items. "He will," she managed. "Thank you."

There were a lot of families at the beach but it wasn't so crowded that they couldn't have a large area all to themselves. They walked toward the sparkling topaz water, their arms brushing as they walked. She struggled, trying not to let his actions cause the edges of her heart to curl with happiness. But it was hard. Everything about him touched the wounded depths of her soul. And then there was the profound and undeniable fact that he would make a wonderful daddy to Kevin.

Could she be falling in love with Levi Sinclair?

"Are you okay?" he asked.

"Yes," she said too quickly. The question echoed in her thoughts. "Here, let me spread that blanket out and you can set the basket on it." She took the blanket from the crook of his arm and shook it to unfurl it across the white sand. Her heart beat rapid-fire and she focused on getting control of her emotions.

This was all happening too soon. She needed time.

And yet the emotions were there.

Kevin raced up, his cheeks flushed with running. "A Frisbee! Can we play?"

"Sure." Levi gave her a curious look. "You want to?"

"Yes, I'll throw it first." She smiled. "You two better spread out," she warned and then laughed as Levi jogged across the sand with Kevin hot at his heels.

Before they had gone too far, she shouted, "Heads

up!" As soon as Levi spun, she threw the disk in his direction. She laughed again at his startled expression when the Frisbee flew straight and true right at him…but just high enough that he had to jump to catch it.

"Great throw," he called as he instantly tossed it toward Kevin, who just barely missed it and had to chase it across the sand. The dogs beat him to it and he had to wangle it from Roscoe's mouth.

"Let go, boy." The gentle giant gave his new toy up. Kevin grinned at them. "I'm going to throw it and see who can get it first," he shouted and then flung the Frisbee as hard as he could.

It wobbled crazily in an arc and she jumped up to try to catch it. Levi jumped too and they collided in the air. His arms wrapped around her and he let her fall on top of him in the soft sand. They rolled, laughing together, and came to a halt with her in his arms, looking up into his smiling face. Her breath caught as his deep, woodsy aftershave wafted over her; her heart kicked hard against her ribs, as if trying to get to his.

"I think we tied on that miss." He smiled, not

acting at all as if he was ready to get up.

"I think you're right. But I jumped first and you tackled me to keep me from getting it. Foul."

He smiled. "Or maybe it was to get you in my arms."

"Mom." Kevin laughed as he stood over her and Levi, grinning from ear to ear. "You almost had it. I got it now."

Jessica had become lost in the moment and now, her cheeks heated with embarrassment as she scrambled out of Levi's arms. "That's great. I really missed it, didn't I?"

"Yes, ma'am, but you tried. And that's what counts. Besides, Levi ran into you. I'm glad he caught you, though."

Levi's eyes twinkled with mischief. "I am too, buddy. I'm sure getting tackled wasn't in your mom's plans." Levi stood and held his hand out to her. "Let's get you up off the sand. I think it's probably time for us to have something to eat."

"I'm starved." Kevin headed to the picnic basket.

Jessica placed her hand in Levi's, feeling the

warmth of his touch as he pulled her up and then gently tucked her into his arms.

He glanced to make sure that Kevin wasn't looking. "I really am sorry. I wouldn't hurt you for the world."

She looked at him. "I know." She moved out of his arms.

And it was true: she knew that Levi Sinclair would never intentionally hurt her. She just had to figure out whether she could risk her heart on the unintentional aspect of that equation. Because Adam would never have intentionally hurt her either and yet he had hurt her deeply when she had lost him.

CHAPTER FOURTEEN

Levi could not believe he had tackled poor Jessica like a linebacker on a pro football team. Or a thug being taken down on the run. If he was hoping to impress her, that certainly wasn't the way to do it. She could've ended up in the hospital. But thankfully she seemed okay. Tomorrow she might be sore, though.

Kevin waited for them on the blanket, eagerly peering into the picnic basket. As they approached, he looked up. Levi's heart tugged at the delight on the kid's face. He was getting pretty used to seeing the little boy happy and he knew he would do anything for

Kevin.

And Jessica.

"You see something in there you like?" he asked.

"Oh yeah, there are some Cosmic Brownies in there. I love them." Kevin grinned.

Jessica sat down on the blanket. "You like anything that has the Little Debbie logo on it."

"I kind of like Little Debbies too," Levi said. "I just took a chance that Cosmic Brownies might be a hit. I think kids usually like those candy things on top of anything."

Kevin nodded excitedly. "I do. I like them peanut butter chocolate thingies too."

"Nutty Buddies, and you like *those,* not them."

"Oh, right. I like *those*. I also like them—I mean, *those*—rice crispy cookies. Yum."

Jessica chuckled and glanced in the basket. "Wait, please tell me that's not filled with snacks only? I'm starting to believe that maybe you two boys are planning to make a meal out of only junk food."

"I brought more than snacks." Levi reached into the basket and pulled out a plate covered with plastic wrap that had a neat assortment of sandwiches that he'd cut diagonally into four small triangular sandwiches.

Jessica looked at him and arched an eyebrow in question. "You even cut them into triangles?"

He shrugged. "Growing up, we always liked it when Mom cut our sandwiches into triangles. I guess the kid in me came out when I decided to do this picnic for you and Kevin."

Kevin giggled. "I'm not complaining. I like little triangles too. Do you have any peanut butter and jelly in there?"

Levi pretended he was insulted. "Of course I do. What kind of question is that, young man? A man has to have his peanut butter. It puts muscle on your body."

He saw the look on Jessica's face watching them and wondered what she was thinking. He wondered whether she struggled at moments like this, watching Kevin in moments that could have or should have been spent with his dad, Adam. Levi remembered many times when his own dad had taken the family for picnics on the beach like this and the fun they'd had.

He couldn't imagine spending those moments with anyone other than his dad. He wanted to gently stroke her cheek and tell her he was sorry that she had gone through the loss of someone she loved. He wanted to tell her that he could make it all right, and yet he knew that he couldn't.

How could he even think she would want to replace what she had felt for her husband for someone else? The question plagued him. He even felt guilty for the fact that he was glad he was getting to share this time with them. *But it was borrowed time…someone else's time.* The thought slammed into him and the reality hit him that the only reason she was here with him was because the man who should be here was dead.

It was a tough reality. It was a moral dilemma for him and suddenly he was uncertain how he felt about that.

Jessica's heart melted as she watched Levi with Kevin. She was in deep trouble. This man was going to be hard to resist. She wasn't sure of anything at the moment except that Kevin needed this.

They ate and giggled and laughed. Levi teased Kevin and tossed food to the dogs and pointed out seagulls and clouds. As the sun began to dip in the sky, he and Levi flew the kite for just a quick moment before the breeze gave out and dusk settled over the bay. Her heart ached, watching them together.

Most of the families along the beach had gathered up their things and headed to the cars. There were just a few scattered people along the long expanse of beach. She realized as she sat there she wasn't ready for the night to end. It was too perfect, too beautiful.

They were gathering up the blanket, getting ready to go home, when a scream pierced the air.

Levi spun and dropped the picnic basket when he saw a woman race toward the water. It was after hours for the lifeguards to be on duty. Jessica scanned the water as Levi started to run.

"Call 911, now," he shouted over his shoulder.

Jessica grabbed her phone and punched the emergency number. Then she grabbed Kevin's hand

and they ran after him; the dogs bounded behind him. Before she could reach the woman, Levi had raced into the waves.

The dispatcher on 911 answered. She quickly told her what was going on and told them Levi had just gone into the water. The raspy-voiced female on the other end of the line was all business as she told Jessica to hold on, help was on the way and that she had the best that there was there helping.

"What is it, Mom?" Kevin's voice wobbled.

Jessica's heart was in her throat. She hadn't been there when Adam had gone into that water to save the family from disaster. She hadn't seen him pull them out one by one, going back again and again. She'd been told by the grateful family but she hadn't been there.

She hadn't seen him disappear beneath the water. But she'd dreamed it over and over and over again.

She had relived that moment in her mind, in her heart, so many times that she didn't want to live through this one. Didn't want to imagine or even think that Levi wasn't going to come up out of that water.

She squeezed Kevin's hand, pulled him into her arms and held him tight as she prayed for Levi's head to come up above the waves. She saw the person in the water's hand waving before it, too, disappeared beneath the water. Her heart nearly stopped beating. *Where was Levi?*

Desperation filled her. *She should go in. She should help.*

But she couldn't leave Kevin. Her son had already lost too much. So she prayed. And then she saw Levi's head pop from the water. Relief washed over her like a waterfall. He had the swimmer grasped in the crook of his arm, the typical life-saving grasp of a lifeguard. Relief, cold and chilling to the bone, filled her. *They were coming in, thank God.*

Her heart lodged in her throat while Levi struggled out of the water, pulling a teenaged boy with him. When he got him to the wet sand, he turned him on his side and patted his back several times. Thankfully, the teen was coughing and coherent. Levi had gotten to him in time. His mother, still hysterical, rushed to hug her son.

Sirens could be heard in the distance as the few people who were still on the beach now gathered round. Jessica had knelt to the sand and held Kevin close as they watched Levi work with the teen. Kevin trembled in her arms and she felt his tears against her shoulder. Felt her own tears flow down her cheeks.

When the police SUV raced across the sand, followed by the ambulance, she picked Kevin up and he clung to her neck, feeling so small in her arms. He was a little big but she held him tightly in her arms and headed toward the truck. They had seen enough. She was thankful that the teenager was okay. Thanked God for it. But she and Kevin weren't okay.

"Honey, it's going to be okay, babe."

He rolled his head back and forth on her shoulder. His wet tears rubbed against her skin. "I thought Levi was going to die like Daddy."

Her heart ached. "He was okay, though. You saw him. He's fine."

Kevin lifted his head and sniffed. "I don't want to lose him too."

Jessica fought off tears. She could not cry right

now. But she knew she couldn't lose Levi either. And she couldn't let Kevin lose him either…

Walking away now might protect them from the heartache that they could suffer if she let them get any deeper in love with Levi.

Love? No—she could not let herself love him. If she loved him, she could lose him. If she let Levi into her heart, he could break it. If she pulled out now, they would hurt but not nearly as horribly as they could hurt if she continued their relationship.

CHAPTER FIFTEEN

As soon as the ambulance pulled away, carrying the very lucky teen to the hospital, Levi went in search of Jessica and Kevin. He found them in the truck, looking less than good.

Sorrow was written on Jessica's beautiful face and in the slump of her shoulders.

Kevin looked small and brokenhearted too. But when he saw Levi, his eyes widened and he held his arms out. Levi didn't hesitate to pull the little boy from his mother's lap and into his arms. Kevin's body trembled as he held him and he met Jessica's eyes over her son's shoulder.

"Hey now, everything is fine, Kevin. Everything is going to be all right," he assured both of them.

"I thought you were going to drown like my daddy."

The words hit Levi like a tsunami and he understood. This had brought back all the pain these two had endured. Of course witnessing the boy almost drown would make this more personal to them. The emotions on Jessica's face made more sense now, given the traumatic loss of Adam.

"I'm sorry I scared you, son." The word slipped out before he could stop it. Jessica looked away, staring out through the windshield into the darkness.

"I wouldn't leave you."

"My daddy did."

"Your daddy was in the water a long time, saving all those lives that he saved. He didn't leave you on purpose." Levi was in over his head. He looked to Jessica; however, she sat stiff as a statue and continued to stare out the window. Worry tore at Levi.

"Come on. Let's get you home."

He put Kevin in the backseat and buckled him in. "Your daddy would be really proud of you, young man. You were very brave. Losing your daddy was very hard. And you have helped take care of your mom and Roscoe all this time. You are growing into a great young man. I didn't know your daddy, but I know that he's looking down on you from heaven right now and he's smiling because you've been so brave."

"Levi is right, Kevin, honey." Jessica turned slightly in the seat so that she could look at her son. In the truck's interior light, he could see the love and concern in her eyes for Kevin. "You've been wonderful and brave and your daddy is very proud of you."

"I want him to be. But I was worried about you, Levi," Kevin said. "I love you and didn't want to lose another daddy."

Levi's heart dropped like a sledgehammer. Jessica's gaze met his and he could not tell what she was thinking.

"It's time to go home." She then turned back to face the front and tugged the seat belt around her, a signal it was time to move.

Levi closed Kevin's door and then rubbed his forehead as he strode around the truck. *Where did they go from here?*

"Is he sleeping?" Levi asked when Jessica came back into the living room after she had laid Kevin down for the night. It'd taken a little while. Kevin had wanted Levi to read a bedtime story to him, but given the daddy comment, she thought it best to dodge that request.

Instead, she had told him that she would do it and she had asked Levi to wait for her if he could. She hated to ask—he was still wet from having gone into the water—but this was important. They needed to talk.

He had a towel wrapped around his shoulders and sat in a chair on the deck, watching the dogs play in the yard.

"He's sleeping. Emotions wore him out more than worry." She folded her arms across her middle, bracing for what she was about to say. "I can't do this, Levi. I can't go through this again. And I can't put Kevin through this either."

Levi stood and walked over to her. "Jessica, don't be rash. You're just upset. I understand if you call this off. But not in a rash, sudden moment like this. You're emotional. It was hard on both of you. I get that and my heart hurts for you. But—"

"No buts. You heard what Kevin said. He called you Daddy and you called him son. I can't—" Her voice broke. "I can't let him get hurt again."

Levi wrapped his arms around her, drawing her close. He felt so good and she rested her cheek in the crook of his neck, needing the comfort…needing him.

"Jessica, I love you. And I love Kevin. I would never let anything happen to either one of you."

He loved her. She fought back a gasp as his words sank in; she stiffened against him and lifted her head. *What was she doing sinking into him this way?*

She needed a barrier between them to fight off the joy that tried to burst through her at his words. "I can't." Despite unbearable desire to lay her head back on his shoulder and to give in to this growing weakness for his touch, she backed out of his arms. She repeated, "I can't, Levi. I hope you can understand."

He stared at her, his expression stunned but concerned. Then at last he nodded. "I'm here if you need me." He stepped from the deck. He whistled for Jaco and walked toward the side of the house and the gate. Her heart screamed no as he disappeared around the corner of the house.

Jessica stood there with Roscoe and then sank to the steps of the deck, eye level with the accusing eyes of the dog. He studied her, as if blaming her for making his friend go away. She had no doubt that when Kevin learned they wouldn't be spending time with Levi anymore that he would look at her in that same accusing way.

Levi was damp, irritated, and his itchy clothes were not improving his mood as he walked into his house and slammed the door. Jaco looked up at him with an anxious expression, as if knowing something wasn't right.

That was the understatement of the year.

Nothing was right.

He'd saved a life, for Pete's sake. That should have counted for something and instead it had been a catalyst for disaster.

He stripped off the wet, offensive clothes and got into a hot shower as the image of Jessica's face and Kevin's played across his mind. He tried to relax as the hot water pounded against his tense shoulders but thoughts kept coming. After telling her he loved her and her telling him she couldn't continue the growing relationship, he hadn't known what else to do at that moment. She was too upset, too distraught. *Would she be better tomorrow?*

He was in over his head, drowning in uncertainty about how to handle the situation. Did you push someone who suffered from such grief? Did you just step back and give her room? One thing he knew for certain: he wanted to do what was best for Jessica.

Even if that meant walking away from her for good in the end.

He'd be the first to admit that he didn't say his prayers like he should, but with his hands on the wall of the shower and the hot water pounding against his tense skin, he prayed for guidance. Because he needed answers and there was no way he could bear making the pain in Jessica's eyes worse.

The next morning, Jessica was so thankful that it was Saturday. She was startled when Kevin bounded into her room and jumped on the bed, with Roscoe trailing behind him. Roscoe watched her curiously from where he sat on the floor.

"Are you awake yet?" Kevin asked, all smiles.

She would never have guessed this was the same sad little boy from the night before.

"I'm awake." She sat up and smiled at him. "You look happy this morning."

"I am, Mom. I been thinking all night long about how Levi is a hero. He saved that boy last night. It was cool. And that's what my daddy did."

"Yes, you're right. And you're not upset

anymore?" Her child never ceased to surprise her. Resilience was the word that came to mind.

"No, Mom. It scared me last night. But just wait till I tell all the kids at school what my new daddy did."

Jessica's heart ached. But this had to stop. "Kevin, you can tell the kids at school what Levi did. But honey, I've told you this already. Levi is not going to be your new daddy. And you have to stop saying that."

Kevin's brows met and his face scrunched with perplexity. "But he is."

Jessica wanted to scream. Uncertain she was doing the right thing, she took his hands in hers and said firmly, "Stop it, Kevin. The only way Levi could be your new daddy is if I married him. And I'm not going to marry him. Do you understand that?"

Kevin yanked his hands from hers and glared at her. "You could marry him. You like him. He makes you laugh and smile, and I saw you kissing him and that's what mommies and daddies do."

"You saw me kissing him?"

"That night after the birthday party when I was

supposed to be asleep. I peeked around the door and you were on the couch kissing."

Jessica groaned. "First, you don't need to be talking to me in that manner, young man. And second, kissing does not mean getting married." She didn't say anything about the laughing and smiling that he was talking about. It was true. She couldn't deny that Levi Sinclair had brought her back to life in so many ways that even her child had noticed it. *What did she say to that?*

She focused on his attitude. "I need you to apologize for talking to me so rudely." *Way to go, Supermom.* Her child was in crisis and she was having him apologize to her for being rude. He was expressing himself. But she didn't know what else to do. She had to figure out a way to get control of the situation. And the only thing she knew was to fall back on telling him to mind his manners.

She might just win Mom of the Year.

Geesh—*not.*

"I'm sorry," Kevin said calmly. He scooted for the edge of the bed. He climbed off and met her gaze.

Then, without another word, he turned and walked out of her bedroom. Roscoe, the big lovable dog, cocked his head and looked at her as if asking what was she doing. She immediately thought of Adam.

Roscoe was Adam's dog. Looking at him now, it was almost as if she could see Adam looking back at her through the sweet dog's eyes.

He makes you happy.

The phrase echoed through her but it wasn't in the sound of the small voice in her head but in the sound of her husband's deep, precious voice. *He makes you happy. He makes you smile. He makes you feel love.*

And he makes me feel fear, she countered. And with that thought, she got out of bed and got dressed. She had a feeling it was going to be a long day.

She was walking into the kitchen when her phone rang. It was Jillian. "Hey," she said when she answered.

"Hey yourself," Jillian said. "How are you and Kevin? Levi called and told me what happened. He's worried about you. Both of you. I'm on my way over. Just want to warn you."

"We're fine. You don't need to—"

"Too late—already in your driveway." The line went dead.

"Mom, Jillian is here." Kevin raced around the hallway entrance toward the front door. He had obviously seen her through his window.

Jessica didn't know what to think. She was glad to see her friend but she didn't need anybody trying to talk her into decisions this morning. Feeling pressed, yet grateful to have someone worry over her, she went to answer the door.

Jillian was all smiles as she talked to Kevin at the door, trying to be upbeat for the boy considering Levi had told her how upset he'd been last night. She'd headed over as soon as she'd hung up from talking to Levi— who had sounded awful himself.

Jillian was glad that Ryan would be working the shift with him today. Her brother was in love—there was no doubt about it—and he needed support right now.

Jillian believed that Jessica was in love too, but she didn't know what the best thing to do was, other than to be her friend and give her support also. Maybe the distraction of being asked to help with the Valentine plans might give her something to focus on. Yes, maybe it was sneaky, but Jillian had a gut feeling this was what was needed.

"Kevin was telling me about last night. That the teen lived."

"And Levi was a hero," Kevin added.

Jessica frowned. "We are so very happy that the boy was safe. I hope he's recovering well this morning."

"He is. Levi went by this morning and checked on him. He was doing good, so they're releasing him this morning."

Shadows crossed over Jessica's expression. "Good. That is so great."

"Can I come in?" Jillian asked.

Jessica blinked, looking flustered. "Yes, sure. I'm sorry, I was just about to make a pot of coffee. Kevin, do you want to go play with Roscoe in the backyard?"

"Yes." He raced toward the back door, with the big dog bounding after him.

Jillian laughed. "They are a pair, aren't they?"

"Two peas in a pod they are." Jessica led the way into the small kitchen that overlooked the backyard.

"Have a seat." Jessica indicated one of two barstools at the small island.

Jillian sat down and watched as Jessica finished getting the coffee brewing. "So really, how are you?"

"I'm…" Jessica leaned against the counter and sighed. "I'm a wreck. That scared me so much last night. I know I'm hurting Levi, but I can't help it. I have to do what's right for me and Kevin."

"So you're saying you're not ready to fall in love. I get that. I'm just worried about you. Levi said you were really upset last night, that the near-drowning really reminded you of when you lost Adam. And please don't get mad at him for calling me. He did it out of worry and concern for you. He said you would be better off if he wasn't here, so he sent me instead."

Jillian tried to gauge the emotions playing across Jessica's face but because it was such an emotional and deep subject, it was hard to tell whether speaking of Levi upset her or whether all the trouble in her expression was from memories of her husband's accident.

"I'm just a mess emotionally. I can't face losing someone again. It takes too much from a person. Jillian, I had my heart ripped out when I lost Adam. People asked me how I got through it and did so well. People said they were impressed with the way that I got through losing Adam. But the thing is, I had a child. I got through it because he needed my strength. I got through it because I felt Adam's strength with me. I got through it because there was no other option. But now, I have an option and it's not to let my heart get broken again. Last night reminded me of where I didn't want to go."

Jillian hurt for her. She knew the heartache that Jessica was feeling. She remembered that day when the doctor told her that the probability of her getting pregnant was almost nonexistent. Remembered the grief that had shattered her that day at the prospect of not carrying a precious child. Her dream. But still, what she'd felt wasn't the same because Jillian had the hope of getting married and the possibility of being able to carry her own child, if she married quickly. She'd had options. Jessica couldn't see that she had options too. Options for a full and happy life ahead of her. If she could reach for the future and not look only back at what was behind her. Maybe it was too soon.

"I understand the fear that you probably are feeling about that. If I was in your shoes, I would probably do the same thing."

Jessica filled two coffee cups and set them on the island. Cream and sugar were already set out. She took the seat beside Jillian.

"Are you not afraid of losing Ryan in the job that they have?"

"There's some worry there. I mean, they are police officers and have to take the oath to protect and serve. But Ryan's job before this one was really dangerous. I mean, he was an undercover narcotics cop. And the truth is, I love him so I can't imagine not marrying him." She took a sip of her coffee, her thoughts whirling.

"What if you lose him?"

"I would rather have loved him and been with him for a short while rather than to have lost him and never gotten to be his wife. See, I had loved Ryan all my life. At least, it seems like all my life. I cannot resist being his wife. No matter what the risk was. And I have a feeling that's how you felt about Adam."

Jessica nodded and looked away. "That's how I felt. Feel. If I had known how it would end, I would've married him anyway."

"I thought so. I want all of my brothers to have that kind of love. To know what my sisters and I have found with our husbands." Jillian laid her hand on Jessica's arm and squeezed. "I want Levi to feel that, to know what that kind of deep, undeniable kind of love feels like. So I respect you for pulling away. If you don't think that that's something you'll feel for him, it will be easier now than later for him to move on. Because I can tell you, Levi has fallen in love with you. He may not have told you that but I can tell."

"He told me." Jessica's voice cracked. "And you're right. He deserves more than I can give him."

Jillian smiled sadly. "Maybe you're right. Only you know that. So are you going to be okay?"

Jessica nodded. "If Kevin doesn't end up hating me over this. He's doing okay this morning. Surprisingly. But he still believes that Levi is going to be his daddy. And I had to be blunt with him and tell him that wasn't going to happen. So it will be strained around here for a few days. We will survive, though. Once more."

Jillian stood and hugged her friend. "It will be okay. I must confess," she said, releasing Jessica, "Kevin really locked on Levi the moment he saw him sitting at his desk the day we took him to the police station. I noticed it right away. Maybe I should not have suggested him for the show-and-tell."

"No, it wasn't your fault. They did connect. I should not have continued to spend time with Levi."

Jillian took a deep breath. "Who knows what was best. Anyway, you have a plan now, and you'll move forward with that and Levi will respect your decision because that's the kind of man he is."

Jessica nodded. "Right. He'll respect the

boundaries."

But Jillian didn't hear any happiness in her friend's statement. "Okay, look, I need to tell you about what's going on at the resort. And this will distract you. We're having a Valentine Bachelor Auction at the resort next Friday. It's perfect since the fourteenth is on Saturday—it should be a great attendance with the dates set up for Saturday night. It's a little rushed, I'll admit, but we decided to do it at the last minute. I have twisted arms and convinced my brothers, including Levi, with a dash of guilt trip, that they should be in the auction."

"A bachelor auction?"

Jillian nodded, trying not to feel guilty. "Yes. Isn't it exciting? The money will go to a charity and the publicity of it will be good for the resort's wedding venue profile and romantic getaway destination. I'm wondering, since you're not going to be interested in bidding on anyone, could you help us out that night? We'll need a lot of help. And it should be fun. But I would understand if you said no." Jillian rattled off her statement fast. "We're really looking forward to it.

Won't you help us?"

She held her breath and waited for what Jessica would say.

"Okay, I guess," she said after a brief hesitation.

"Great," Jillian exclaimed, feeling very, very greasy at the moment. This might be the worst sneaky trick she had ever done. But as far as she was concerned, it needed to be done. And only time would tell whether it was right or wrong.

CHAPTER SIXTEEN

Levi had managed to stay away from Jessica for four days. Four long, unending days. By Tuesday, he was going crazy, not to mention the fact that Friday just happened to be the Valentine auction. That thought only brought him heartburn.

Especially when he'd walked into the office that morning to find two pound cakes and a chocolate pie on his desk.

And Betty Lou leaning against the doorframe of the dispatch room, with her arms crossed and a grin as wide as the Grand Canyon across her face.

"Mornin', Chief. Looks like you're going to be eating well over the next few days. I'd be watching that waistline of yours. You don't want a little paunch showing when you get up on that runway on Friday. You'll need to look trim and maybe show off those abs of yours if you're planning on getting top dollar for yourself. You know, to benefit the charity and all."

"You should be a standup comedian, Betty Lou," he grunted. "Where did these come from?"

She hooted with laughter. "Three different women came in here this morning around seven thirty and dropped them off. They were all trying to get here first and hoping you'd be on duty, so they came before dropping their kids off at school. I thought catfights were going to break out when they met in the front room. Yikes, they did not like seeing each other. There was estrogen bouncing off these walls, I can tell you that. You dodged a bullet."

This was ridiculous. "This is out of hand."

"What's out of hand?" Max walked in the door. "I hear I've missed some excitement while I was out of town."

"You made it back—glad of it, brother." Levi crossed to give his brother a hug. He had begun to worry about Max because he'd been gone longer than usual. Still, he didn't even bother to ask what he'd been doing; he knew Max couldn't say a word about it.

"Oh, we are glad you're home, and you've made it back in time to see what I figure will be the catfight to end all catfights on Friday night." Betty Lou gave Max a hug and patted his chest. "Mmm-hmm—hard as a rock. The gals will like that." She smiled. "I'll let your brother explain all the cakes and the pie and estrogen." With a grin, she strode back into her office.

Max looked at Levi. "Do I dare ask what's going on?"

Levi grimaced. "Have you not heard? Our sisters have lost their minds. They're having a bachelor auction for Valentine's at the resort this Friday, and you may not know it yet, but now that you're back, you'll be on the auction block along with the rest of us."

Max's gaze narrowed. "I haven't heard anything so far. I got in late last night. But after what I've been through for the last several days? Cake and a date sounds really, really appealing right now. I might have to give our sisters a hug."

Levi glared at him. "You are not helping the situation, man. You're willing to take a date with whoever pays the highest price for you?"

"I'll suffer through."

"Right. If you had gals gunning for you like I do right now, you might not be so enthusiastic. Those cakes are from a bunch of single moms—oh, forget it. You're dadgum lucky you live outside of town where almost no one can find you, or you might start finding a pile of cakes beside your fence."

Max laughed. "What bee has got up your shirt?"

Ryan walked in, took one look at the desk and laughed. "This is great." He walked over to get a better look at the desserts. "What do we have here? Chocolate, chocolate, and chocolate. They all look good to me. And to answer your question, Max, Levi is the most wanted bachelor in Windswept Bay at the moment."

Levi did not want a date with anybody but Jessica. "Have at it, guys. Eat your hearts out. I've got rounds to make."

Not even looking back, he headed out the door with their laughter following him. It was heck when a man couldn't get any peace at work. He'd backed off and kept his distance from Jessica all these days but maybe that had been the wrong thing to do. He'd had a small hope that she would seek him out. Make the first move. But that hadn't happened. Jillian had told him that she was making it okay. That she just wasn't ready for a relationship right now.

And so he had stayed away. But could he keep it up?

Jessica didn't think the last bell of the day was ever going to ring. She was so ready to go home. To hole up and pretend her heart wasn't hurting. When there was a small tap at the door, she looked up from where she was grading papers. Lana was reading the kids a story over in her area of the classroom. They liked to take turns doing story time. It gave each of them a little time to get caught up when they took turns. Today,

Jessica struggled to concentrate on the papers and was relieved to have a distraction as she walked to the door. Dawn Lively, who owned the florist shop, stood in the hall with a vase of red roses. She smiled at Jessica.

"Oh, hi, Dawn." It was Valentine's week and so she'd been seeing Dawn's delivery girl delivering flowers several times today and would probably be here many more times until Friday. But this was the first time she'd seen Dawn delivering flowers herself.

"You must have the wrong room—"

A twinkle lit her eyes. "No, not at all. These are for you, Jessica," she said brightly. "I've heard rumors that there are a lot of women wishing they'd gotten these flowers from our hunky police chief. Happy Valentine's Day. And lucky you."

Jessica could do nothing but accept the vase as it was pushed into her hands. They were beautiful. It had been a very long time since she had gotten roses. Butterflies tickled through her. "Thank you but—"

Dawn was already walking away. "Enjoy," she called over her shoulder. "Oh, I hear he's up for grabs at the auction Friday night. You might want to get in on that action."

Jessica cringed and stared back at the gorgeous, deep red roses. They were perfect, each and every one.

"What's that, Mom?" Kevin called.

She spun and found him and the entire class watching her. Including Lana.

Her friend cocked her head to the side and grinned. "Yes, indeed—what is that?"

Questions came from all the kids in a rush. They jumped up and raced across the room; she found herself surrounded as questions flew.

What was Levi thinking?

"Are those from Chief Sinclair?" Lisa asked, suspiciously. "My mom took him another cake this morning. She is going to buy him at the auction."

Meg stuffed her little hands on her hips and glared at Lisa. "My mom is going to buy him at the auction on Friday. For a Valentine's gif, she took him a chocolate pie this morning. My favorite. He will love it."

"My mom cooks better than yours," Lisa snapped.

"Girls, no fighting," she said, shocked by

everything that was transpiring. "Stop this. Everyone take their seats."

Lana stood behind everyone and bit her lip to keep the laughter from escaping. Jessica shot her a warning glare that only made her friend clamp a hand over her mouth to hide her laughter. Thankfully the bell rang at that very moment.

The next little while was spent getting the kids out the door and to the bus stop and the pickup line. To her joy, Jessica did not have after-school duty since she'd had it that morning. Therefore, she hurried back toward her room, where Kevin would be waiting. With the flowers.

Her son had asked about Levi all week. She'd finally given up and refused to acknowledge that he was continuing to insist that Levi was going to be his daddy. That's all that she knew to do. *And now Levi had sent flowers.* It was going to confuse Kevin.

Grudgingly, a tickle of happiness at seeing the beautiful flowers seeped through her. She fought to ignore the feelings. *Levi had stayed away all week, so why send flowers now?*

She'd been trying to ignore everything about Levi but her thoughts had made him tough to ignore. And since she'd agreed to help with the Valentine auction, the tension had been growing.

Why had she agreed to help when Jillian had asked her?

Jessica was not dumb. She knew that Jillian had an ulterior motive and yet she still was going to help. She came up short as she entered her class room and found Kevin leaning on her desk staring at the flowers. He grinned excitedly.

"Momma, Levi sent you flowers?" Kevin asked, with hope in his eyes.

"Yes, he sent me these flowers and I'm not sure why."

"Because he loves you," Kevin quipped happily. "I told you he loves you."

She counted to ten. "Levi is just being nice." It was lame but what else could she say? She refused to tell her son that he was right. His declaration of love moved over her as she thought of him on the deck.

"He loves you, Momma. And what's a bachelor

auction?"

Could she just curl up in a dark corner for a moment? "They're having a fun thing on Friday evening for adults—an auction for Valentine's Day dates."

Lana walked in. "An auction is where you have something and people try to buy it and the one who offers the most gets it." Lana leaned against Jessica's desk.

Jessica decided she would hurt her later.

"What's a bachelor?"

Lana grinned. "A single man."

"Like Levi?"

Lana nodded. Jessica edged close to her so-called friend and kicked her lightly in the ankle. Lana yelped and shot her a startled glare, to which Jessica mouthed, "Cut it out."

"So Lisa's mom and Meg's mom are going to try to win Levi?" Kevin then added anxiously, "You have to win him, Momma." He crossed his arms. "He sent you roses. It's probably a sign that you should help him. Lisa's mom is scary."

If it wasn't so important, it would be funny. "Kevin, I'm not going to bid on Levi. And it's not like marriage or anything. It's for a date."

Kevin glared at her. "Donald told me that his mom and dad went on a date and got married two days later. Just so you know, dates lead to marriage."

"Kevin, you are too smart for your own good." She glanced out the window and saw his friend playing on the swings while he waited for his mom to get through in her classroom. "Look, Tom is on the swings waiting, so don't you think you need to go get some exercise?"

Kevin shrugged. "Okay, but this is serious. Just so you know." He stomped out the door.

Lana's lip should be bleeding by now, to keep from laughing she had clamped down on it so many times today. She was biting it again as Kevin strode out of the room and her eyes were bright with laughter as she looked at Jessica. "He's right," she chuckled.

"This is not funny, Lana. My child is going to have a breakdown over all this. He's living in a delusional world. And you aren't helping."

"Jessica, maybe you're the one living in a delusional world. You have not been yourself this whole week. Ever since Friday when all that happened. When you were telling me about it—it's just not right. I get that it's hard. And I honestly don't know what to tell you about Kevin. He has gotten this infatuation with Levi—of course, there are several women and their children who have infatuations for him also. That poor man is going to need help at the auction. It should be very entertaining. You could just save him from the vultures if for no other reason. Heck maybe I should if you aren't."

"You're going?" Jessica asked.

Lana's eyes widened. "Are you kidding? I wouldn't miss it. They are charging a cover fee, and for good reason—that resort is going to be packed. Nearly all the teachers are going. And between you and me, there will be several teachers putting their bids in on those Sinclair brothers. Those guys are hot."

"Are they bidding on Levi?" Jessica's gut tightened.

Lana shrugged. "I don't know. Not that it matters

to you."

Jessica watched her friend walk across the room to her desk, sit down and pull out her paperwork. She had a sly smile on her face.

"This isn't funny, Lana."

"It is a little," she countered. "And come Friday night it could be one dickens of a show."

Friday evening, Levi arrived grudgingly at the resort fifteen minutes before six, just as his sister had instructed him to do. His brothers were all hanging out at the poolside bar area of the resort, along with the handful of other bachelors who had agreed to this ridiculousness.

To his surprise, they all looked at ease, standing around, talking and laughing and mingling with the ladies who had started to arrive. Like Max had said, they were just here to have a good time.

"Good time my foot," Levi grumbled as he took a spot at the edge of the pool house, next to the sea life mural that Cali's husband Grant had painted.

Leaning against the painting of a playful seal, he did not feel playful at all. *Nope.* Arms crossed, he scanned for a glimpse of Jessica. He spotted her helping Jillian take names at the table where the women evidently signed up to get the privilege of bidding on the bachelors. It reminded him of the setup when he'd adopted Jaco. And he knew what the pup must have felt like in that cage that day.

He resisted going to talk to her and remained firmly ensconced in his surveillance position.

The cakes had continued to come to the office. About ten of them sat on the coffee bar but he hadn't eaten not one piece of those desserts. And didn't plan on it, either. He saw several women who had dropped off their cakes and he fought the urge to back out of this and head home. Suddenly, Jessica looked up and her gaze found him.

Even from this distance, he saw her breath catch. His heart exploded with love.

Time. He just had to give her time. And be prepared for her to walk away again.

To his surprise, she left the table and came his

way. His heart felt as if it were going to break out of his chest. He had missed her.

"Hi," she said, almost shyly. "They told me you were going to be here. It looks like you'll have a lot of people bidding on you. That will be good for the charity."

"Right. How are you?" He didn't give a hoot about the charity right now.

"Okay. Making it. Thank you for the flowers. I wish you hadn't."

"I worried about you all week," he said. "But I stayed away like you wanted. Not like I wanted."

She glanced away and then back. "Maybe you'll meet someone tonight. I'm fine. This is for the best."

"Jessica, I'm not in any hurry. I love you. With all my heart," he added. "I will not meet someone tonight. I'm only here because of my sisters. I know you're not ready to hear that I love you but I do. This is not a race, though. Love is patient. I'm not going anywhere."

She looked down and he wanted to pull her in his arms so desperately that it hurt. Instead, he picked up a strand of hair from her shoulder and felt the soft gossamer between his fingers, just needing to touch her in some small way.

"You can't wait for me. I'm trying to tell you I can't go through what I went through again. Everybody told me I handled Adam's death so well. But they didn't know inside my heart was a mess. I can't do it again."

Levi stared at her and it finally started to sink in. "I'm never going to win your heart, am I? I never stood a chance competing with Adam." He was competing against the dead man and he always would be with Jessica. Adam was a hero, a great man, a great father, and he had been a great husband. "I don't know how to compete against that—against a perfect dead man. And I hate even saying that because it sounds awful. But I have to tell you, Jessica, I have never, ever envied anyone before but I envy Adam. If he loved you like you love him, he would not want your warm, vibrant heart lying in that casket with his body."

Her mouth fell open in a gasp. "I need to go back and help," she said, her voice weak. And then she turned and walked away.

And he let her.

"*Wow.*" Jake stepped out from the side of the building. "That was intense. You okay, brother?"

"No, but it doesn't matter." Levi saw the concern in Jake's eyes. Jake played hard, enjoyed life and lived it to the fullest. He was not ready to settle down and of all of his brothers, Levi thought he would be the last to settle down. Jake put a hand on his shoulder and squeezed.

"You picked a tough problem. She's not looking like she's going to come around anytime soon. Are you going to bail on the sisters? I'll let them know, if you want."

Levi frowned. He wanted to bail but he'd promised all of his sisters. Jillian, Cali, Shar, and Olivia all expected him to participate in their fiasco. And he was a man of his word—though this was pushing his boundaries.

"I promised them I'd be in this thing and I will be. Like it or not." *But never again.*

Jake's expression turned skeptical. "I have to tell you that with that scowl on your face, I'm not sure you're going to be doing them a favor. Your fans might not even be bidding with you looking like an angry pit bull."

Levi grunted. "That would be the best end to my night."

"I'm looking forward to my date. Not sure who's going to win me, but I'm betting I'll go higher than any of you guys," he teased. "Especially with you wearing that expression—but I get it. You've got problems." Jake sobered. "Really, though, are you going to be okay?"

"I'll live, so rest easy and go have a good time."

"Will do." He gave his shoulder a pat before he headed over toward the crowd. He was sidelined by a tall blonde before he got too far away. And Levi saw several other women edging toward him. Levi might not be happy about this but Jillian did have a good idea to promote the resort. He saw cameramen arriving and groaned.

What had he gotten himself into? He wished he could've said to heck with his integrity, loaded up and gone home.

CHAPTER SEVENTEEN

Jessica was a nervous wreck when the auction started. They had had a podium erected beside the pool for each of the single guys to stand on as the auction began. She had to sit there with her list of bachelors and know that Levi was going to be number five of twelve.

The auction was a family affair. Cali and Grant, along with Shar and Gage, would be watching the crowd and taking bids. Olivia and BJ would be on the podium, acting as announcers, with BJ doing the actual auctioning. Jillian and Ryan were coordinating, while

Ryan was also ready to take control if there was trouble. She'd heard him joking with Levi's brothers that the crowd could get unruly when it was Levi's turn and all the first-grade moms came out to fight.

It might be a joke but the thought gnawed a hole in her stomach.

Plenty of women had asked her whether it were true that Levi was up for bids. They'd heard the rumor that she and Levi were getting married and she had to set the record straight more times than she cared to.

And now they had news station coverage too. The camera crews hovered about and Jessica wasn't sure what to think about all of that.

She should have stayed home.

She'd have an ulcer before the night was over.

Some of her students' mothers were ready with their bidding number—that Jessica had had to assign them and then write on their paper-heart bidding paddle.

Lisa's mom, Trisha, looked like a million dollars…or a Victoria's Secret model. She wasn't sure why the woman wasn't married. If she really wanted to be, she definitely had all the attributes to get attention. But then, Jessica had also dealt with her in class and knew that she was pretty hard to handle. Maybe that was the problem.

Or maybe Trisha had gotten a raw deal—who was Jessica to judge?

She watched Trisha locate Levi and head over to talk to him.

Levi immediately, while talking, inched his way toward his brothers. As if being alone with Trisha was not something he wanted.

His movement was blocked when other females, some of them mothers from her class and others she didn't recognize, drifted toward him. It was evident that the women of Windswept Bay had a thing for their police chief.

But then Jessica understood why all too well. And it wasn't sitting too well with her, thinking about any of them spending time with him.

"That frown is going to stay there." Jillian walked up to the table.

Jessica frowned deeper. "I'm really not in the

mood to be teased."

"I see that. Remember, it's just a date—no worries," Jillian said.

Jessica heard Kevin telling her dates led to weddings. He was the authority after his playground buddy had told about his parents. "He is free to date whomever he wants."

Jillian smiled. "Well, I better go help. It's about to get started. Are you ready to write down the bids?"

Jessica picked up her pen. "Ready."

And so it began…whether she was ready or not.

Olivia stepped up to the microphone as the master of ceremony. Levi had been told that they'd wanted Jillian to do it since it was her idea but she hadn't come out of her shell enough to get up in front of a crowd. So Olivia had agreed to do it and volunteered BJ to be the auctioneer.

"Welcome to the first, but hopefully with your help, not the last of the Windswept Bay Resort Valentine Bachelor Auction. We are going to have a very fun night—"

Some whistled and many women laughed, having a good time as they teasingly waited for the twelve men to take their turn on the auction block.

"Now remember, these are dinner dates, ladies. We're not auctioning off anything but dancing and dinner. Remember, almost half the lineup of men are my brothers, so no hanky-panky." Olivia shot her brothers a smile but Levi had a hard time finding it funny.

"Come on, man." Trent leaned in so only Levi could hear him. "Get with the program. You're not about to face the firing squad. It's a bunch of women wanting to pay for dinner with you."

Levi focused on Trent as Olivia continued to talk. "You and Jake are enjoying it enough for me and all of you at the same time."

Trent chuckled. "Jake said you were a goner and I believe it. Walk away, buddy. It's not worth it. This is a fun night for a great cause. If your heart is somewhere else, then just bow out. The sisters will understand."

Levi was tempted but in the back of his mind he

had a small hope that Jessica might decide to bid on him. "I promised. And like you said, it's just dinner."

"First up, my brother Trent."

Trent grinned at him and the other guys. "Got to go, fellas. Watch the bidding and weep."

"You'll be weeping when it's my turn," Jake said, and the crowd laughed.

"I'll give you a hundred for dinner with that hunk," shouted out Francine Degan, a great-grandmother in her eighties with a great sense of humor.

Levi and the other bachelors laughed when Trent's pride took a visible hit.

"I'll up it to one twenty-five," Patsy Post, Francine's buddy, called out and waggled her eyebrows.

BJ grinned. "Well, we have our opening bids, and they are setting a great pace for the charity donations. Who'll give me one thirty-five?"

Levi had to admit this was looking as if it could be entertaining…at the expense of watching the others get picked off one at a time. When it came to him, he almost hoped Patsy or Francine would win him but Trisha Mosley had her eyes on him. He had a bad feeling she'd come with a blank check in hand.

"How's it going?" Lana scooted into the seat beside Jessica. "Sorry I'm running late. I got tied up. Did I miss anything?"

Jessica shot her a glance. "Trent, John, and Alex have been bought. The two great-grandmothers on the front row are driving up each bid so the charity is doing great." She turned the numbers so Lana could see them.

"Oh my, that puts me out of the ballgame. I'd bid but my teacher's salary doesn't allow me to splurge three hundred dollars to five hundred on a date. Sheesh. These gals are serious."

Jessica's stomach churned. "Yes, and well, look at Trisha. She has had her eyes glued to Levi. And look at that dress. Her cleavage is showing almost to her navel."

"I thought you were not interested anymore?"

Lana drawled slowly.

BJ called out Jake, who was one ahead of Levi.

"Well, look at her. She's going to—" She had to stop talking as bidding on Jake broke out fast and furious. The good-looking guy had a great sense of humor and he hammed it up as he strode out onto the platform. He flexed his muscles like a body builder would and scanned the room with a bring-it-on attitude. It was more than obvious that Jake Sinclair liked the ladies and was in this for the fun of it. And Francine started the bidding off at five hundred dollars, which Patsy quickly upped to five fifty.

"You young gals need to back off and let me have this hunk," Patsy warned, looking around the room, grinning.

The two older women were having a great time driving up the bidding. But instantly, a tall, lean, very defined and in shape woman lifted her bidding paddle.

"Six hundred," she called. Then there were a flurry of bids in increments of ten, then twenty, and finally she ended the bid and won with seven hundred dollars.

"This is crazy," Lana grunted. "I obviously need a different profession."

"Me too." Jessica wrote down the winning bid. Her nerves were shot now. She glanced at Levi. He glanced her way; his jaw was set and though he'd laughed several times at the expense of the other guys, she knew everyone in the room who was paying attention knew the woman in the tight black dress, letting it all hang out, had her eyes on him. And she hadn't made a bid on anyone else.

Jessica told herself he was a big boy and could handle this. Told herself she couldn't risk losing someone else again.

"You're going to break that pen if you squeeze it any harder," Lana pointed out. "Trisha is getting her dinner and a movie date. Look at that determination in her steely gaze. Yikes, she's like a vulture ready to eat him alive."

Jessica shot her friend a glare. "You are not helping."

"Hey, I'm just calling it like I see it."

BJ called out, "Okay, ladies—and now for our

local police chief, Levi Sinclair. Any takers on this keeper of our law and order here at Windswept Bay?"

Patsy beat Francine to the punch with a five fifty bid. Francine countered with six hundred and a couple of women countered with six fifty and then six seventy-five.

Trisha calmly waited. "Eight hundred dollars," she said, her voice as thick as molasses.

"Holy smokin' tortillas," Lana said, her Texas twang ringing out in the room.

Jessica's chest seized up as though she had a horrendous case of heartburn. And she dropped her pen. *Eight hundred dollars.* Sweat beaded on Jessica's forehead and her mouth went completely dry.

Trisha was going to get Levi.

Levi groaned, feeling like raw meat about to get eaten by a lioness. Trisha had a predatory gaze locked onto him and he knew he was doomed. *He was a man*, he told himself, *the police chief and he could handle himself.* This was a charity thing but he had no desire to be tangled up with the woman who clearly had some over-the-top infatuation with him.

Suddenly, another woman jumped up and shouted eight twenty-five.

"Eight hundred ninety-five," a small blonde he knew had dropped off a pie called out.

Trisha glared at her. "Nine hundred."

A redhead joined in. "Nine fifty."

Nine hundred and fifty dollars for a date with him? Had they lost their minds? He tried not to look at Jessica but couldn't help himself. Her eyes were wide and her jaw set as she stared at him and then back at the women. She was not scribbling numbers as she'd been doing on the other bids. And he felt for her as he saw her pale and heard Trisha say one thousand dollars.

"One thousand dollars," Jessica gasped.

He stared at Trisha and she smiled at him.

"I want this date. And he's worth every penny," she said, smugly.

BJ waited a moment. "We have a bid of one thousand dollars. Who'll give me one thousand twenty-five?"

No one spoke.

"Going once. Going tw—"

"Two thousand!" Jessica yelled, jumping up and waving the clipboard.

Levi's heart thundered. He knew on a teacher's salary she didn't have that kind of money. "What are you doing?" he growled, glaring at her. He didn't want a date with anyone but her but this was beyond ridiculous.

"I'm winning you." She shot a defiant glare at Trisha. "I'm getting this date."

"Drop it, I'm out of this. A date with me isn't worth that kind of money."

"Two thousand five hundred," Trisha said, glaring at him. "You can't just bow out."

"Three thousand," Jessica growled. A pin dropping could have been heard in the room. Jessica looked back at Levi. "And I'm not looking for a date. I'm looking for a lifetime."

"What?" Levi took a step toward the edge of the platform. Joy and disbelief jolted him.

"And that's worth whatever price I have to pay." She dropped the clipboard on the table and took a step toward the platform.

He laughed. His heart swelled with love for this woman. "Honey, you can have everything I have and am and it won't cost you a cent."

Trisha growled and then stomped her foot. "Fine. Take him," she huffed. She threw her paddle to the ground and stormed out of the room.

"Sold—" BJ started to say but Levi wasn't listening. He had stepped from the platform, scooped Jessica into his arms and was heading away from the crowd. He didn't stop until he was on the beach, with the moon shining down on them and the soft sound of the waves taking the place of the ridiculous bidding.

"You know I won't hold you to all of that." He wanted nothing more than to kiss her and hold her for as long as she'd let him.

"I know. But, Levi, I realized back there that I don't want to lose you. I lost Adam. And I pushed you away. In essence, I lost you and it was of my own doing. I love you and I want a life with you…I might have some ups and downs but I can't lose you when you already have my heart."

He hugged her and buried his face in her hair, breathing in the sweetness of her. "Baby, I'm all yours. From here to eternity."

His heart full of love, he kissed her. Something he knew he would never get enough of…

Jessica locked her arms around Levi as his kiss filled her with longing and hope and joy.

She loved and lost and had been blessed to have shared that with Adam. Now, she let go of her fears and melted into the knowledge that her love for Levi and his for her would overcome any fear, every time.

When he pulled back and looked into her eyes, she saw the gorgeous romantic moon reflected in the depths of his gaze. "So, where do we go from here?" she whispered, unable to get her full voice.

He smiled. "Will you marry me? As soon or as far away as you want it…I just need to hear you say yes." He set her on her feet but continued to hold her in the circle of his embrace.

"Yes," she said, instantly. She cupped his face

with her hands and kissed him. "We can work the details out as we go. But, right now, I know a little boy waiting at the babysitter's who'll want to know he was right all along."

Levi laughed. It filled her with joy and she knew his love was a gift. A gift she couldn't turn away from.

"I love that kid," he said, and she knew it was true. "Let's go tell him. But you need to know that I'll never try to take the place of his real dad."

Tears came then. "I know. But he and I both have room in our hearts for both you and Adam. I know that now. And I think Kevin has known it all along."

He traced the side of her face with his fingertips. "Thank God." He led her toward the resort, headed toward the back entrance, and bypassed the rowdy auction area where bidding was still going on.

"Do you think I need to go back and keep up with the bids?"

"Nope. Someone else will fill in. We've got a boy to see and plans to make so I can put a ring on your finger."

Jessica nodded. Her heart was too full for words.

"I can't wait."

And she couldn't…suddenly life seemed brighter with Levi by her side.

A few minutes later, as they told Kevin they were going to be married, Jessica thought her heart couldn't take any more joy on. But it could.

"I told you that you were going to be my new daddy!" Kevin threw his arms around Levi's neck as tears stained his cheeks. "I knew it."

Watching them, Jessica felt peace flow through her. She felt Adam's smile, warm and dear and forever in her heart.

Levi held out an arm; she stepped into the circle of his embrace and wrapped her arms around him and her son and the new life they were about to begin together…

EPILOGUE

Max watched from the sidelines as Levi and Jessica left the Bachelor Auction spotlight. He was glad for them. They were both settled and seemed like a great match. He let his gaze rove around the gathered crowd as the excitement and disruption of Levi and Jessica's declarations of love raced through the crowd.

He'd been a little shocked at the dollars being thrown around for these bids and wondered if now they'd die down to a normal price range. He wasn't looking for a date with a rich socialite or a wealthy grandma. He'd had a rough mission that was still bothering him and he just wanted a night out…he could have easily gotten his own date but his sisters had seemed overly excited about this auction and so here he was.

Of course, he and his brothers knew part of their sneaky push was for exactly what had just happened between Levi and Jessica. And it was nice that it had worked out. It could easily have backfired but he'd been watching his brother and the man had been about to go crazy wanting to jump off that platform and snatch up the woman he'd fallen in love with.

Love-Max had been thinking about that for a lot lately. And last week while he'd been raiding a hideout of a top-ranking terrorist organization he'd almost been killed…he hadn't told anyone, and wouldn't. It was part of his job description. But in that moment, when he should have been detached and focused, he'd thought about what he'd missed out on. What he'd sacrificed for the good of his country and he'd wanted more...

He focused on the chatter around as BJ called out

another bachelor and the auction resumed. Was he really ready to pull back? To start thinking about more?

His phone beeped with the tone that was dedicated to his commanding officer. He pulled it from his pocket and glanced at it. Duty called.

He moved toward Shar who was standing closest to him.

"Hey, sis," he said, wrapping an arm around her waist and giving her a quick hug. "Sorry, but duty calls. Good luck. See you when I get home."

"Shoot," Shar growled. "Already? You just got back?"

"And I'll be back again."

She frowned. "I know. Still, it's hard every time we watch you go."

"It's nice to know I'm missed."

"And loved. Be safe. And get back here quick."

He winked then not taking the time to tell the others goodbye he slipped out and headed toward the parking lot. Shar would explain. And he'd see them when he got back.

In the parking lot he spotted his brother, Cam, running late obviously.

"Hey, Max, what's your hurry?" Cam called, spotting Max as he altered his course and jogged toward him.

"Cam, you made it. Slick move to be late for the auction."

Cam shrugged. "I couldn't help it. What are you doing—dodging a date?"

"Nah, I got called out. The auction was almost over but I need to report for duty immediately. If you hurry, maybe you can take my place." Max knew getting up on that stage was the last thing his older brother would want to do. Cam ought to do it though, he was old enough that settling down was probably on his mind. But knowing his cowboy brother like he did Cam was probably going to eventually find him a wife in Texas where his ranch was.

"I think I'm fine." Cam grinned, then grew serious, his gaze drilling into him.

Cam knew Max couldn't say a word about where he was going and might not even know at this moment where he was heading off to. He'd told Max plenty of times that he was proud of him but worried for him while at the same time he understood that Max loved what he did.

Max was glad they'd run into each other but he felt the moments ticking. He had to go.

"Look, I hate to run, but I need to get there. As usual, I'll let all of you know when I'm back stateside." He stepped forward and gave Cam a hug. Felt the bond of their brotherhood and was grateful for it. He felt Cam's arms tighten hard before he let him go.

"You watch yourself, little brother."

He knew Cam wouldn't bother to tell him to be safe. He understood that wasn't always a possibility for Max with the top-secret missions Max was involved in.

"I always do. Tell Levi to watch out for my pig while I'm gone." He grinned, turned and started jogging back toward his truck.

"You and your pig," Cam called. "That's just not right. You need a wife to come home to, not a guard pig."

Max turned, jogging backwards, grinning. "Not the right time. But you, on the other hand, are all set up for a wife, with your ranch in Texas and your advancing age."

It was true. Max—was the youngest Sinclair brother and Cam was the oldest and they had an ongoing joke between them, Cam teasing he was a baby and him teasing Cam that he was an old man.

Cam laughed. "Who knows. Maybe I'll be married by the time you get home."

"Then you better hurry. This is supposed to be a short mission. In and out. Gotta go. I'll meet the new missus when I get back." He laughed over his shoulder as he jogged off. Then he stopped and turned back. "Hey, Cam," he called, serious now. "Really, take care of yourself. Glad I got to see you before I left."

And then he jogged the rest of the way to his truck and hopped inside, cranked it up then drove out onto the road. He had a bag ready in the back of the truck for quick deployment. Levi would check on his place and Charlotte. He had everything lined out. Max had no strings, no obligations to hold him back. He was a good soldier. And that had always been enough. Moments later, as the chopper lifted off into the dark sky carrying him and his unit his gut tugged and he felt unsettled. Something wasn't right…he wasn't sure if it was a bad feeling about this mission or the last one. But maybe it was just the gut feeling that it was time to change something in his life…to start thinking in longer terms than from one mission to the next.

Cam watched Max leave and fought to ignore the unease that churned in his stomach. Max would be back. His brother knew how to take care of himself, still, tonight he was glad they'd run into each other before he left. Turning, Cam moved back to his truck and climbed back in to grab his keys and lock the doors. His brother had great instincts, a plus in his line of work, and in the short moments they'd talked Max had hit the target that had been nagging at Cam for the last few months.

He was ready to settle down.

But the last time he'd checked, it took the right

woman to settle down with to make the equation work out right. As of yet, he hadn't found her. The right woman.

But he was open to meeting her any time she decided to show up. Though he doubted it would be before Max got home. He climbed from the truck, glanced back toward where he'd watched Max's lights disappear into the night and fought off the wave of unease. Max wouldn't want him to worry. Taking a breath, he headed toward the resort and hoped like the dickens that his sisters didn't try to put him up for auction.

CHAPTER ONE

C am Sinclair pulled into the parking lot of his family's resort, now run by his sisters. He was running late…but it couldn't be helped. He turned the engine off and as he started to get out of the truck, he spotted his brother Max jogging across the parking lot. Cam hopped from his own truck. "Hey, Max, what's your hurry?"

His younger brother saw him and altered his course toward him. "Cam, you made it. Slick move to be late for the auction."

Cam shrugged. "I couldn't help it. What are you doing—dodging a date?"

"Nah, I got called out. The auction was almost over but I need to report for duty immediately. If you hurry, maybe you can take my place."

"I think I'm fine." He knew Max couldn't say a word about where he was going and might not even know at this moment where he was heading off to. He was proud of Max and worried for him at the same time, but Max loved what he did.

"Look, I hate to run, but I need to get there. As usual, I'll let all of you know when I'm back stateside." They hugged.

"You watch yourself, little brother."Cam didn't bother to tell him to be safe. That wasn't always a possibility, he had a feeling, with the top secret missions Max was involved in.

"I always do. Tell Levi to watch out for my pig while I'm gone." He grinned.

Cam watched him jog a few steps. "You and your pig. That's just not right. You need a wife to come home to, not a guard pig."

Max grinned. "Not the right time. But you, on the other hand, are all set up for a wife, with your ranch in Texas and your advancing age."Max—being the youngest Sinclair brother at twenty-nine and Cam being the eldest at thirty-three—liked to rub in the four-year age difference.

"Who knows. Maybe I'll be married by the time you get home."

"Then you better hurry. This is supposed to be a short mission. In and out. Gotta go. I'll meet the new missus when I get back." He laughed over his shoulder and jogged off. Then he stopped and turned back. "Hey, Cam," he called, serious now. "Really, take care of yourself. Glad I got to see you before I left."

And then he jogged the rest of the way to his truck and was gone.

Cam watched him leave and fought to ignore the unease that churned in his stomach. Max would be back. Turning, he moved back to his truck and climbed back in to grab his keys and lock the doors. His brother had great instincts, a plus in his line of work, and in the short moments they'd talked Max had hit the target that had been nagging at Cam for the last few months.

He was ready to settle down.

But the last time he'd checked, it took the right woman to settle down with to make the equation work out right. As of yet, he hadn't found her. The right woman.

But he was open to meeting her any time she decided to show up. Though he doubted it would be before Max got home.

Lana Presley left the Valentine Bachelor Auction at the Windswept Bay Resort dateless, but smiling. She hadn't gone to find a date. She'd gone to see whether her friend, Jessica, would get one. And thankfully she had. Love was a wondrous thing…not that she was looking for it. But she still enjoyed the romance of it all when it worked out.

It was the crashing and burning that went along the way to finding love that she herself was weary of.

Still, the Sinclair sisters should be excited for themselves because their bachelor auction had been a huge hit. Especially for her friend Jessica and Levi Sinclair. Her friend had been worrying her lately. Lana knew that Levi was good for her, so Lana had been rooting for the two to get together.

The fact that Jessica had come out of her shell and taken a chance on loving again was wonderful. Lana didn't know what went on after they left the auction together but she was excited to hear all about it. And she hoped they were now officially an item.

Lana had to admit that the auction had been an eye-opener. All the guys had been really having a great time and the Sinclair brothers had been so good-natured about the whole thing that just watching them had been entertaining. But one brother had been missing—the one she was curious about, Cameron—or Cam as they called him. He lived in Texas and owned a ranch. He was a cowboy rather than a beach boy. Not that any of the Sinclair men looked like boys but they had all settled in their hometown on the shores of gorgeous Windswept Bay.

Lana had heard some of the teachers talking about the brothers in the teacher's lounge at school. And she'd heard his name come up a few times. And because she was from Texas herself and she and her five brothers had been raised on a ranch, she had been curious about the brother who'd moved to Texas to become a rancher. Not that she was interested in any way, just curious about him. She'd had one too many dead-end relationships with cowboys to be thinking anything other than just plain curiosity about the man.

She'd actually moved to Windswept Bay to get away from cowboys—including her brothers and her dad. She needed space. She had begun to build her own life here and she really liked it. Though she did miss riding her horses. She had heard there was a small stable in town on the island; she planned to check it out tomorrow and was excited about the prospect of riding again.

She'd parked her truck at the back of the parking lot and finally reached it. Climbing inside the cab, she inserted the key and turned it. Instead of the engine firing up, all she heard was a dull clicking noise of a dead battery.

"No, come on." She groaned and tried again—as if

that would change the fact that she had a dead battery. She'd known her battery needed replacing and she hadn't stopped and changed it out. She was giving herself a good scolding when she noticed the truck lights go out not too far away from her. Only then did she realize that the truck parked across several parking spaces was pulling a horse trailer.

In between scolding herself, she wondered who was driving the rig. If there was one thing this Texas girl knew, it was to take care of her business. She should have stopped by the auto-parts store and picked up a battery right after this had happened the first time. Certainly the second time she'd had to get a jump from someone. But she hadn't and now she was serving the consequences, as her dad would say.

She shot a glance over at the truck but the parking lot lighting made it hard to make out who was driving.

The big rig made her think of her brothers and her dad—ranching and hauling horses or cattle was part of the job. Taking care of your business and equipment was also part of the job. They'd be giving her the dickens right now for letting this happen and stranding herself.

She leaned forward, popped the hood release and then exited the cab. She glanced over at the truck once more, curious who was driving it and staying at the resort. She strode to the front of the truck—which had also been used for hauling animals. She reached for the release lever and then pushed the hood up. She pulled out her phone, found the flashlight button and then grabbed the grill with one hand and placed her boot on the front fender. She was too short to do anything standing on the ground. She pulled herself up, leaned under the hood to peer into the dark cavity as she aimed her light on the engine.

"Do you need some light?"

"What?"Lana yelped, jumped and slammed her head into the hood before she lost her balance and slipped from the bumper. She would have fallen if strong arms hadn't caught her.

"Are you okay?" the man asked, holding her securely against his hard chest.

"Am I okay," she muttered, rubbed her head and glared at the man."Don't you know to warn a gal? You don't just walk up and scare a person." She struggled to get out of his arms. Her head throbbed, she probably had a goose egg the size of Texas on her forehead thanks to him.

"You're sure," he asked, sounding skeptical but setting her on her feet.

"Positive," she grunted and immediately backed away from him while still massaging her throbbing forehead.

"I apologize," he drawled, sounding truly concerned.

His tone wasn't completely Texan but sounded totally cowboy. She inhaled and tried to calm down as she focused on him. He tugged his hat off and it gave her a better view of his shadowed face. Whoa…she sucked in a breath. The resemblance to all the other Sinclair brothers was unmistakable so she knew instantly who she was looking at.

Cam Sinclair.

Oh, my…her thoughts stalled, her gaze caught by penetrating eyes glinting in the low light.

"Are you okay? I was trying to help. Not injure

you."

He was tall, with striking features—even in the shadowy lights she could more than tell the man could cause traffic jams and break hearts too. Which she knew more than enough about.

She got a grip on her imagination. "I'm fine. And I'm sorry I got so upset. But just so you know, next time you come up on a woman in the darkness, give her little warning." She scowled, completely unsure why she was so irritated.

He flicked on his phone light and held out his hand."Let's start over. I'm Cam Sinclair. And I'd like to take a look under your hood if you'll let me."

Lana lost her voice.

"Are you okay?" he asked again. "You look pale in the light."

"Um, yes, I'm fine. Sorry."What was wrong with her? She'd seen plenty of good-looking cowboys in her day.

"So can I?"

"Can you what?"

"Look at the truck?"

She blinked and gave herself an imaginary kick in the jeans. "Yes, sure."

"Are you sure you're feeling all right? You really do look a bit strained."

She nodded, feeling quite silly actually.

He moved to the truck and leaned under the hood, shining his light into the engine compartment."This is a mighty big truck for a small woman."

She stood on her tiptoes. Yes, she had big tires that hiked the truck up higher than a regular truck. "It's no bigger than yours over there."

He lifted his head to look at her. "Do you haul with this truck?"

"Not these days. But yes, I have."

He nodded, his expression thoughtful as he took that info in. She didn't elaborate. Although she knew who he was, she didn't feel the need to tell more.

He focused on the truck, jiggled a few things, took the cap off the radiator and replaced it. Checked the oil and then studied the battery. "I'm thinking it's the battery, so let's give it a try."

"That would be great. It's done this before."

"You'll need to get a new one tomorrow." He cocked his head to the side and met her gaze with serious eyes that she couldn't make out the color of in the dim light. "Okay. Getting stranded isn't a good thing. Your husband or boyfriend can fix you up."

"Yes. Sure. Thank you." Her pulse bucked like a rodeo bull and it was irritating as fire. "And, it's all on me. I'm single and free and I'm the one who didn't get the battery."Now why had she let that out? Too much information.

Reminder to self: Cowboys are off my list of allowable attractions and I'd do well to remember that.

He didn't say anything, just tipped his head and strode off.

Lana watched every step he took.

Yup. The man looked fine in his jeans and boots. Shoot. This would not do. Not at all.

Cam moved his truck forward. The lady was irritated and had him wanting to smile. She definitely had a mind of her own. He hadn't meant to scare her but she'd grabbed his attention the minute she jumped from the seat of the truck. He'd watched her march to the front of her vehicle and push the hood open as if she knew what she was doing. When she'd hoisted her small self up onto the front bumper, he'd started moving as fast as he could toward her. He'd been so intent on offering her help, he hadn't thought about scaring her. He felt really bad about that—but when she'd fallen into his arms…he'd been glad he'd been there.

She was a spitfire, it was easy enough to see, and he recognized a Texas twang when he heard one. This was no Floridian. He pulled his truck up close enough to hers so the jumper cables would reach. Then he hopped out and got them out of the steel gear box mounted in the truck bed.

"I'm sorry, I didn't mean to be rude," she said when he walked back to her. "I'm Lana Presley. It's nice to meet you. I'm acquaintances with your sisters."

"Acquaintances?"He studied her.

"I'm fairly new in town and have just met them briefly."

"I see. Well, welcome to Windswept Bay. I can tell by your accent that you're a Texan. Are you any kin to Marcus Presley of the Presley Ranch?"In the darkness, it was hard to read her expression but he was pretty sure she stiffened.

"I might be. Is there a problem?"

The coolness in her tone startled him. He shrugged, curious about her now more than ever."No, ma'am, no problem." He applied the cables to each truck. "You can go crank it now."The lady clearly didn't want to talk about any relation to the Presleys of Texas.

She headed away and in a moment, the engine started. He removed the cables from the battery. His work was done. But he wasn't ready to say good-bye.

"Thanks."She came back to the front of the truck.

He pulled the hood down and closed it. "You're welcome. I'm glad I could help."

She pushed her wavy, dark hair behind her ear. She was pretty in a simple, no-nonsense kind of way. She had a wide mouth, almost too wide for her small face, and a square jaw that lifted in defiance, he'd learned, when she was tense. It had lifted when he'd asked about the Presley relationship. Now it lifted again and he found himself wanting to smile. He had a feeling that despite her size or her calm beauty that if she was riled up, she'd have a temper.

"I didn't mean to sound rude before. I just don't really know you."

He tipped his hat. "I understand. A lady can't be too careful. You need to get this battery fixed tomorrow."

She cleared her throat; he thought she was going to say more but instead she nodded and turned to go.

"Maybe I'll see you around while I'm here in town." He wasn't shy and she interested him.

She paused at the open door of the truck. "Maybe. But probably not. I was just here tonight for the bachelor auction."

"Ah, I see. Did you get one?"

In the shadowed light, he thought she cringed. "No. I didn't come for one."

And with that, she got in her truck and with a slight wave, she backed the truck out of the parking space and drove away.

Cam watched as Lana Presley pulled out of the parking lot. She had not been exactly rude and not exactly happy to be around him either. All he had done was help her. Despite his interest, there was no denying that she'd been a little prickly—and clearly not interested in anything he had to offer.

So why was he still mulling over thoughts of her as he entered the front entrance of the resort in search of someone from his family?

He wasn't sure whether the Valentine auction was over or whether anybody would still be around but just in case, he headed into the resort. Hauling horses from Texas to here was a long haul and he hadn't made it in time to help his sisters out. He hated to say it but he wasn't sorry he'd missed being in the auction. He was here on business, though they didn't know it, and he really didn't have time, even for a charity, to go on a date. He also wasn't real keen on the idea of being bought as a date.

He spotted his sister Cali entering from the back courtyard entrance of the resort.

He was the oldest son and she was the oldest daughter, so the two of them had always been close.

Her expression brightened the moment she saw him. "Cam, you made it late but you made it! It's so great to see you."

"Hey, sis. Good to see you too." He hugged her and saw her husband Grant coming through the sliding doors. "Grant, I see she didn't auction you off." He laughed and he shook hands with his friend.

"No." Grant grinned as Cali wrapped her arm around his waist and smiled up at him. "She didn't auction me off, but they got everyone else auctioned off. It was a night to remember."

Cali smiled. "Jillian had a great idea. I just hope none of the dates turn into disasters."

"That wouldn't be good." Cam grimaced.

"No, it wouldn't. But the best part of the night was that Levi got bought by Jessica. Remember the lady he brought to Mom's birthday party?"

"Yeah, he brought her and her little boy, I remember. So she bought him?"

Cali smiled. "She did. It was awesome and

romantic. And made the whole evening worthwhile. Which was Jillian's ulterior motive in the whole episode."

"Well, that's great. Levi's starting to get to that age where he's looking to settle down."

Cali's expression brightened even brighter "So are you at that age?"

He was older than Levi and his twin Trent. "Yes, nosy sister, you heard correct. I am really starting to think about my future. And all my sisters getting married and being so happy has influenced me."

She laughed."Yay."

Grant tugged her close. "Good to know. If you ask me, it's the smartest thing I ever did."

Cam looked to his good friend, who still owned a ranch next-door to his in Texas. "We both know it's the best thing that happened to you. You've never looked happier."

"You're right about that."

"You should have made it to the auction and gotten this ball rolling." Cali's eyes twinkled.

He laughed. "I think I can find my own way."

"Okay, good luck. So weren't you making a horse delivery or something?"

"I had some business I'm hoping to finalize tomorrow." He glanced at his watch. "I hate to run but I've got a trailer full of horses I need to tend to. I'll be around."

"Where are you boarding the horses? Are you staying at Mom and Dad's? You're more than welcome to stay with us."

He decided there was no reason not to tell. "I'm taking them out to Bess's horse stable down on the beach road."

"Of course, I should have known that but I heard she sold it suddenly. And that last week she left town and went to live with her sister."

Grant eyed him suspiciously. "Did you buy that place?"

Cam laughed, unable to keep his secret any longer. "I did."

"Oh my goodness," Cali exclaimed. "I can't believe it. Are you moving here?"

"You are full of questions. When I was here for

Shar's wedding, I dropped by to check on Bess. I hadn't seen her in a while and just thought I'd say hi. She taught me a lot about horses growing up and helped fulfill my dream of becoming a cowboy. While I was there, she asked me if I'd ever consider buying her place. She was ready to retire and so we struck a deal."

"I think that's wonderful. Mom is not going to believe this. Why didn't you tell her? Or us?"

"Because I wasn't certain Bess wasn't going to pull out of the deal. It's a sentimental sale. I only wanted her to be happy, so if she had decided at the last minute to keep the stables I didn't see any reason to get Mom and Dad's hopes up."

"I understand. Well, this is so exciting."

"I think it's great," Grant added. "I'll have to come out and ride some."

"I'll be going over it this week. Come out when you have time. I just stopped in to check on how the auction went, but I think I'm going to head over there now. It's been a long day."

And he was ready to see his place. When Bess had

asked him whether he'd be interested in the place, it had surprised him. But then, he'd looked around and been startled by the possibilities that he began to see. And the legacy that he had from Bess's patient lessons had meant the world to him. He didn't want to take the chance of some corporation coming in and buying this prime piece of property and doing away with the horses. That had been Bess's only stipulation: it would remain a stable. And that had suited him just fine.

Now he just had to decide how he was going to manage it from Texas.

More Books by Debra Clopton

Windswept Bay Series

From This Moment On (Book 1)

Somewhere With You (Book 2)

With This Kiss (Book 3)

Forever and For Always (Book 4)

Holding Out For Love (Book 5)

With This Ring (Book 6)

With This Promise (Book 7)

With This Pledge (Book 8)

With This Wish (Book 9)

With This Forever (Book 10)

With This Vow (Book 11)

Check out Debra's Other Series

Cowboys of Dew Drop, Texas

Sunset Bay Romance

Texas Brides & Bachelors

New Horizon Ranch Series

Star Gazer Inn of Corpus Christi Bay

Cowboys of Ransom Creek

Texas Matchmaker Series

About the Author

Debra Clopton is a USA Today bestselling & International bestselling author who has sold over 3.5 million books. She has published over 81 books under her name and her pen name of Hope Moore.

Under both names she writes clean & wholesome and inspirational, small town romances, especially with cowboys but also loves to sweep readers away with romances set on beautiful beaches surrounded by topaz water and romantic sunsets.

Her books now sell worldwide and are regulars on the Bestseller list in the United States and around the world. Debra is a multiple award-winning author, but of all her awards, it is her reader's praise she values most. If she can make someone smile and forget their worries for a few hours (or days when binge reading one of her series) then she's done her job and her heart is happy. She really loves hearing she kept a reader from doing the dishes or sleeping!

A sixth-generation Texan, Debra lives on a ranch in Texas with her husband surrounded by cattle, deer, very busy squirrels and hole digging wild hogs. She enjoys traveling and spending time with her family.

Visit Debra's website and sign up for her newsletter for updates at: www.debraclopton.com

Check out her Facebook at: www.facebook.com/debra.clopton.5

Follow her on Instagram at: debraclopton_author

or contact her at debraclopton@ymail.com